Nuha

Some Dreams are Too Pretty to Live

Nuha

Some Dreams are Too Pretty to Live

Somaya Iqubal Khan

GenNext Publication

ISBN : 978-93-8022-313-1

Price : ₹ 180

First Published, 2017

Published by

GenNext Publication
5, Ansari Road
Daryaganj, New Delhi-110002
Phone: 9811692060
E-mail: gennextpublication@hotmail.com

Printed at: G. Print Process, Delhi.

Cataloging in Publication Data—DK
Courtesy: D.K. Agencies (P) Ltd. <docinfo@dkagencies.com>

Khan, Somaya Iqubal, author.
Nuha : some dreams are too pretty to live / Somaya Iqubal Khan.
pages cm
Novel.
ISBN 9789380223131

1. Indic fiction (English) I. Title.

PR9499.4.K43N84 2017 DDC 823.92 23

Dedicated To

Mithi and Maaz
As you both grow up, people will ask
about your real mother and sympathize
Don't let them, because you have
two mothers and they are real

Foreword

"We all have our own tryst with destiny as we set out to pursue our respective dreams. Often, we encounter our own stumbling blocks along the way. Some aspirations are fulfilled, while some continue to elude, leaving us disenchanted. Somaya's story, however, is a true testament to the age-old saying 'What doesn't kill you only makes you stronger.' Having gone through the trauma of losing her sister, her best friend, and other subsequent upheavals in life, it requires sheer courage for her to regroup herself emotionally to lead a meaningful life. Nuha's story draws inspiration from Somaya's relentless struggle followed by her determination to never let adversity decide her fate. It's refreshing to see a young middle-class Muslim girl from Bihar defying all odds to carve a niche for herself. Nuha is not just Somaya's story but will chime with the stories of almost every reader, who hasn't had a chance to narrate their own tales."

Rifat Jawaid, Former Editor, BBC
Founder, Jantakareporter.com

"Ms. Somaya Iqubal Khan is a new generation story teller who has transcended the limits set by society for a 20 something to venture and succeed at something as intense as story telling. She has done a good job at it with her first book, ***Blue Bangles*** getting critical acclaim. has always been fascinated by relationships and how they unfold themselves in today's times. Her journey with her own youth, her own relationships and those around her inspires her to write profusely on how these impact the mind. Particularly weaving a compelling story of a girl who finds herself enmeshed in a web of circumstances that at times create more trouble in her paradise and at times help her to realise her dreams. The story in this Book talks about how a person is the the result of various circumstances he/she is surrounded with. The book strongly argues that one's personality is a result of circumstances and choices one makes. I understand from the effort and beauty in Somaya's work that it shall make for a delightful read and I wish her all the success with her first novel."

Dr Rashmi Jain
Jamia Millia Islamia

"This novel," Nuha–Some Dreams are Too Pretty to Live" coming from a young author-her second attempt after her book of poems "Blue Bangles"is emotional and inspirational.

This simple story will be an insight to the readers about people with mental issues, their needs and why their behavior fluctuates to the extremes. And the book somehow combines being timeless, placeless, and yet firmly relevant to us all, because of it's sheer brilliance.

What distinguishes this book is the fact that Somaya is incredibly well informed, and a personal determination shines through every word; and yet Somaya writes with the beauty of poetry."

Prof. B. Manchanda
Associate Professor and Head-Corporate Affairs
Jagannath International Management School, New Delhi

Nuha

Oh I just got astounded as this realistic writer came up to me with the news of her second book and this time the subject is greater and I am sure better! Somaya,as I have known her and her writing skills-is not only passionate about her life but also how she can reach out to the world and heal every soul herein with a touch of light from the warmth her heart and her words. In a world where eveyrything is carried out with machines and devices,human feelings are in the edge of turning materialistic and unworthy too. However,as a part of the same big world we are all equally responsible to let in emotions and bonds have bigger places than things that can be easily brought and sold. Somaya has this unique brilliancy of throwing light into the current situations of the era. I wish her all the luck and charm to make "Nuha" an inspirational guide for all her readers and let her words heal the heavens and oceans for good.

Keep your spirits high

You wonder girl..!

—Sonam Gill

(Woman of Substance-2015
Miss "Axom Jiyori/Daughter of Assam"-2013
Social Activist- Stop Acid Attacks)

Hey Nuha!

Remember me? We have met before...

Where? Everywhere...

I searched for you time and again. I used to see you crying somewhere, sometimes alone, sometimes with people, sometimes in books, sometimes in kitchen, sometimes travelling, sometimes strolling...always occupied' always silent!

Kudos to Somaya who has brought you infront of so many excited readers, listeners and friends.

Nuha...is "us" dear ladies...

Nuha is an ached heart, a troubled mind, a wandering soul, she is a friend, a companion, an observer, a listener, a mother, a wife, a sister, a daughter...and a little herself for a little while, she is the troubled heart that pines for peace and the tormented soul that seeks refute, she yearns for love. I am ready to travel with her and discover myself; I invite you to travel along. Let the journey to womanhood continue, let the inspiration and the experience continue, let more such writings continue...

Nuha is every woman, listen to her, because if left unheard the silent scream might pierce the heart to pieces.

My best wishes to the woman who voices every woman. Good luck Somaya Iqubal Khan, after having heard the tinkles from Blue Bangles' it's time to hear a story that lets the mind speak from heart and lets the heart listen to the mind

Sana Fatima
Research Scholar
Department of English
Aligarh Muslim University

Prologue

You have exactly two options when life hits you hard, to give up or to fight back. When you give up you lose life and when you fight back you learn life. That was what exactly happened with me a few years back. I was a regular person, living life like most of us, friends, family, college, career, ambition and dreams. Until one day when a phone call changed my life forever, it brought the news of my eldest sister, she was burnt alive.

The reality was too harsh to live when I started weaving a world away from this world....

In attempt to run away, I found myself fighting when,

Writing pulled me out of depression
Social work gifted me the purpose of my life
And heartbreaks taught me Love

I came across many people asking I love the person, but he/she is not ready to be with me or left me or moved on. What should I do?

The one, who will love you, finds comfort in your company and respects you, will be with you

You will not need to abuse, chase and stalk in the name of LOVE

No, that is no love; those things are your low self-esteem, lack of self-respect and non-existence of your life's purpose

Be dignified enough to prioritize yourself, your life, career, family and loved ones.

They have invested their lifetime raising you and you owe them more than anyone in this world

Acknowledgement

Allhamdulillah! To my father and mother, this is for you, had you have not believed in me I wouldn't have become the woman I am. I always aspire to become the woman you are Ammi. Allah has blessed me with such a wonderful parent like you both.

To my sister Sanauwer who has been my lifeline, everything that I am or ever will be is your gift to my life.

I might or might not have been a great sister but I love the strongest pillars of my life, my brothers Kaifi, Ishaan, Aatif, Taufique and Isa. And to the constant of my life, Ravi and Vijay, thank you for being there like pole stars.

I take immense pleasure to thank all the wonderful people who contributed to my book, writing foreword and extending their support in my work. Thank you Rifat ji, Rashmi Ma'am, Bhushan Sir, my lovelies Sonam and Sana.

I wish to extend my gratitude to all my friends who have been the constant support and motivation in my life, Neeta, Sangeeta, Rishi, Saurav, Ashish, Priyanka, Samreen, Puja, Arpita, Amit, Yatish, Vicky, Piyush, Manish, Abdul, Sanjeet, Ravi, Nitin, Asrar, Nikhil, Abhinav, Panda, Roshan Bhagya, Gaurav, Albina, Saani and all my classmates from Jamia. Thank you Hanzala and Talha for your help and Upisha for giving a wonderful photograph for the book cover. And Sabah, you made me realise the value of my work, thank you for inspiring.

Also, I would not fail to mention Faizy, thank you for showing me the other side of the life and the importance of finding a purpose of one's life.

May Allah bless you all and may love prevail. In shaa Allah!

— x x x —

Chapter - 1

Adel and Nuha

It was 12 am and I was brushing my teeth vigorously as if the gums would cry and teeth would bid goodbye to their roots. What do I do, break my head against the cardboard divider of my PG room which is not even a wall to say or just run away in the dark streets of Bengaluru and get lost in the silence of the midnight. I can't talk about it, who would have time to listen to my least comprehended state of mind and why would someone care enough to give a rat's ass to my mammoth sized problem. I decided to sit and write, what else could I have done, I was hurt.

And I wrote:

"Just the last night I was denying the trip they had planned for the weekend, they knew it well that I can't travel; I have cold feet in the name of traveling and long trips. Of them most importantly he knew everything. How I panic to the mere thought of this entire thing still he fought with me for the past one week so that I agree to go. It is like fulfilling once personal desire by walking over other's disability. Friday night we assembled at Neel's place, it was nine of us. Neel, Abhi, Panda and their girlfriends Kavya, Dhiya, Zoya respectively, and Neel's elder sister, Lakshita. Neel, Abhi, Adel and I were from the same school and were batch mates. We were friends but we never thought life would bring us all here in the same city and so close to each other. Most of them were software engineers and placed in different IT companies. Adel was still searching for jobs and Neel was thinking about his career plans after engineering. Adel was the only one left without a job and that was frustrating for him, I knew he had big plans for himself but he was not getting the right start. Engineering has become just another degree which is now sold in different private colleges at various rates; it has certainly degraded the quality of education and mechanised human thoughts. Or you can say, the market is so over flooded with these engineers that joblessness is apparent. Well, Adel was adamant to take me to the trip because all his best buddies were accompanied by their girlfriends, and he wanted the same, so he forced me and I did.

Adel and I were together for the last nine months, it started when we finally hit each other in the alien city of Bengaluru as work brought me here, we gradually came in touch with all the Josephites, (school friends) Adel and I knew each other as we shared the same school, St. Joseph's School, Bhagalpur, that would be like knowing for 10 years and coming this far we started dating. Back in school days I was the least desirable girl of the batch, no guy would ever have looked at me with those eyes that would have made a girl blush and I always went unnoticed. Not to be regretted as we were all in the age where physical beauty attracted the brain because then, a tornado of hormones controlled who we are drawn towards and I possessed none of the parameters, no good looks, no lady lumps, no great academics, nothing that would set me apart or draw any attention. Rather I was a duff, for I had the prettiest girlfriend about whom every other guy dreamt of. Although I seemed ugly but ugliness do not stop you from having a crush on the most beautiful guy in your class. Yes, beautiful, wouldn't call him handsome, he was fair like a maiden with dark black eyes, little lips, bulky body, on the fringe of obese and a great dancer. Girls were all around him, and he was all around in my thoughts. I liked him to the extent that I could never ever look at him directly in his eyes, or stand around him, used to change my path the moment I saw him coming in front. I never confessed but my actions made it so evident that the entire school came to know about it, he did not ignore me but banked upon it and counted me as one of them, on his lady fan list. Occasionally shooting me a romantic message or dedicating a romantic song. I would listen to that whole day long lost in every word of the song. But that castle in the air thing came down as soon as it was built when my prettiest friend revealed the truth; those songs he dedicated to me were sent to all the girls in his network and not just me, came as the first shock. I was undesirable but not foolish; I could have never been one of them. So little by little he lost the charm and my respect. That is where it ended for me, my first heartbreak.

Look where am I carried to, I had no intention to bring this up, but it is impossible to ignore it when you are thinking about where it all started, first heartbreak. So my point was how Adel came in my life, he claimed that he did had a soft corner for me even in the school days but he was too occupied with pretty girls to think about me. And I chose to believe it, we were grown up now, that's what I thought after completing my graduation degree, work life, career planning, the serious relationship was all on a checklist of the grown up. Now, love was more than just pretty looks and attention, it was about mutual understanding, care and concern for each other, commitment to living life together. Adel gave me all these and I couldn't ask for more, I fell for the deal immediately. It was like he was waiting the entire life, just to meet me, it was surreal to believe the affection and care he showed to me, where I became his entire world. His day would start with picking me from my paying guest dropping to my office and ended with having dinner together, spend some time, meet common friends around BTM and by 9 he would drop me back to my paying guest.

This was what life was and this is what everybody's life turns out while managing work and relationship, it was a new place for me but I had not to worry as I had his back always. He cared for every tiny thing of mine and I could only feel blessed. He was like a blessing, an angel for me, my three times meal was more important to him than his own, it was not like he just asked about my meals but he made sure I ate on time. He cried when I was in pain, he looked after me when I was sick, he was there in my needs like a mountain, he was worried when I was tensed, he wouldn't sleep if I couldn't sleep, he made my smile the reason of his happiness. Any girl would adore him for the kind of man he was, with whom someone could get married and live their life. But just like every best thing has the darkest side there was something that was not all happy with us. A perfect man in an imperfect woman's life would no longer be the perfect man.

I was imperfect for many reasons, you would know me gradually. Like this very particular incident, I was supposed to be normal like all the girlfriends of my friends, enjoy the trip and make him feel loved like he wanted to be. But I was not in my normal state, I feared everything, trips, long distance, travel, new place and more than I could enjoy, I had jitters in my body by the mere thought of it. How could they have understood this, they were all sane people and I was the only insane one to be dragged to the trip. On Saturday morning we woke up at 4 a.m. and I gave a last try to stop myself from joining the trip but in vain, he was literally yelling at me for being so stupid and abnormal. He constantly gave me examples of how mean I am and how worthless a girl I am, not fun, not enthusiastic and certainly not a girl to be loved. It made me cry and I felt suffocated in my own body, how badly I wanted to be anyone else but not me I wanted to be normal like normal girls and give him the happiness he deserved. My heart cried and cried and I hardly realised in all these it's just becoming weaker day by day. I tell you internal pain, tears which are not shed becomes a permanent scar on your heart which hurts throughout your life.

We boarded the traveler that was booked, the driver was over enthusiastic about everything, he was explaining the route and other things to be taken care, how you need to be very cautious at the Tamil Nadu border and we need to make things fast as we will be returning the same day. The Hogenakkal fall was 180 km in Dharmapuri district and one of the fierce waterfalls of Karnataka of river Kaveri. They collected the snacks to eat, chips, cakes, biscuits and chocolates. Girls packed their bags with quick makeup tools, lip gloss, fragrance, kajal and everything that was needed to beautify them. I checked my bag for all the essentials too, my anti-anxiety pills, anti-depressants, digestive syrups, headache tablet, medicine for vomiting, anti-allergic pills, and hand sanitisers. I was ready as they were, only that I lacked the zest with what the entire crew was overflowing. Once again Adel had pushed me to a place where I don't belong anymore, and all I did was watch girls and their enthusiasm, all dressed in their best, skin toned under the layers of foundations and eyes accentuated with kohl, lips pinked in the gloss, they looked beautiful. Not to forget the blush on their cheeks as when the eyes of their lovers fell on them, they bloomed like a spring flower. I always seconded this part of the girl's life, of course, they are meant to look beautiful and what If a stroke of makeup give them confidence enough and add to their loveliness, it is worth it. Those girls reminded me of how I once used to be, dressing up, dolled up and walking as if I own the world was the thing I was best in. I knew everything, from the perfect winged liner to the contouring of the face, from carrying a backless red carpet gown to wearing summer shorts. But that has become the story of the past as now I do what Adel wants me to, he did not want me to wear western dresses, he did not want to fake myself with makeup. He always asked me who do I want to impress now, why do I need to work hard to look good because he is already there in my life and he loves me for what I am. I was never convinced but anything for his love, for his love was something that had become more important to me than anything in this world.

I was dressed in a salwar kurta with dupatta and wore no makeup. Oh, Bengaluru weather was such that I had to carry a jacket and a shawl on everything that I wore. Even though dressing up has been my first love I cared less about it now and he also claimed he found me beautiful, I wondered how because someone had told me I never look beautiful without my smile. Anyway, everybody took their respective seats with their partners, chit chatting and looking at each other's eyes, Adel came and sat next to me, I had taken the corner seat in the middle of the row as I knew back seat give more jerks and front seats had the risk in case of any accident. He held my hand and had assured nothing bad will happen all you need to do is just enjoy the trip, people and us. I was relieved a bit with his nice words but my mind was always on alert, and by the time he tried to look at me with his loving eyes, my mind had already travelled to the valleys of infinite worries and consequences that might lead to because of one carelessness, like what if the vehicle tumbles down the cliff, what if the heavy waterfall carries us away with its current, what if we are drowned in the Hogenekkal falls, what if now, right now I get anxiety attack and I would need immediate doctor attention and there would be no hospital to save me, what would I then do, my mind was cluttered with all these worries and I noticed how he had already given up looking at my eyes and talking to his friends turning away from me.

I was still at ease, at least I do not have to do something out of his expectation because showing my love had become a tedious task for me, my mind was never mine, how would anyone expect me to love someone in that state. Suddenly Zoya, (Panda's girlfriend) got up and in her designed tone she asked all of us to join for Dumb Charades. It is a good game but nothing interests me when my mind is cluttered with speculations about what may go wrong.

The entire journey was like merriment on wheels, they danced, sang and made jokes that I hardly understood or you can say I didn't pay enough attention to understand it. I looked outside to the perfect scene of mountains and green fields on the way, it was beautiful, nature is beautiful but for me that deserted land looked ferocious, I couldn't see the immediate life signs, no people, no shops, no hospitals, what would I do if something happens to me, where would I seek help, that scenic beauty hit me hard on my face and I rested my head on Adel's shoulder. It was the only place I felt secure and in no time fell half asleep, I could still hear their voice of enthusiasm in my head, Adel covering my already covered body with a scarf, I could still feel everything, the cool breeze on my face, the occasional sun strikes on my face escaping the crossing branches of the trees lined both sides of the highway. Sleeping was the only time my mind wouldn't wander uselessly to make me worthless and hopeless, it was always peaceful and satisfying. By the time I opened my eyes, I found no one in the van, that was when I freaked in fear and ran towards the gate, I saw Adel coming running towards me and I was sweating in my jacket, he reached to me and held me tight, I asked,

"Why did you leave me alone?"

"No baby, you were sleeping I thought it's good to not wake you up"

"But what's wrong? Have we reached the place?"

"No, we still have 5kms more to go, it's just everyone liked this place, wanted to be photographed and get refreshed."

"Okay, you can join them then"; I pretended that I did not need him, while in my heart I was too scared to be left alone even when they are just a few meters away.

"Would you like to drink something, coconut water", he asked

"Yes. That will be okay", he knew that too, I do not drink anything preservative, or roadside water, it's the coconut water only that I found to be safe and hygienic.

I sipped from the shell while he was clicking photographs cracking jokes with them, they were sitting right in the middle of the highway and getting pictures with different poses and all the while I looked in awe, how daring they are, they fear nothing, that is what life is about, living every moment. I was ashamed of myself, of my incapability, how my thoughts and actions have become my disability; I was not living life but fear in every moment.

After the halt we got to our seats to cover next 5kms and finally reach our destination, this time, Kavya sat beside me, she wanted to start a conversation and when someone tried to do this I usually felt crippled, I didn't want people to question my fear, my worries, and my behaviour, I screamed within, 'please don't uncover me, let me be comfortable in the little black box that I am.' I never liked to be exposed or become the talk of the group. She smiled at me and I smiled back

"So why didn't you come with us for the photographs", Asked in her friendliest tone.

"I was sleeping, didn't feel like going."

"Ok, but Nuha, do try to have fun no, enjoy with us, look how beautiful this place is and we all are there."

Was she making fun of me, I thought but no she was not she was just hitting me hard on my face with reality and I replied in my forced zestful tone, "Of course, I am liking everything, much better now."

She held my hand and raised it as if we discovered something after years of research, or maybe I have won some tournament. The fact was I was still a loser pretending to be another loser.

We were at the gate of Hogenakkal falls, it was bustling with half naked tourists ready to take the plunge, the scenic beauty was breathtaking, a huge green mountain stood like the boundary of the world, like no one can ever know what does it hide behind its massiveness, the entire pathway that leads to the entrance was covered with shops on both sides of the roads, a self-sustained flea market of hats, shorts, swimwear and other essential that would be in demand. There was jewellery made up of beads and shells that were probably made by the locals there. And what stole the hearts of masses were the fresh fried fishes served on the banana leaves. There was small fire set on the patches where ladies sold fishes fried in chilly powder, turmeric and salt. It looked red hot and must be tasty had I have tasted it a bit. How could I, I feared I might get allergic to fishes and shouldn't try something odd at such a place. Everybody had left their shoes and left it in the van, I was the only one walking with my shoes as insects and reptiles were my biggest fear, it was developed over a period of time when an insect bit me just after a few days of my visit to Bengaluru, my entire body reacted with red boils and I had the experience of hell when Adel had rushed me to the hospital in my panic state and doctors were just too worried because my panic had doubled the effect of poison in my body. Adel was continuously reading surahs, duas and was holding me close, had he not been by my side then, I don't know what worst could have happened. He had saved my life and I owe my life to him, there can't be anything I wouldn't do for him. So here I was, accompanying him defying my fears, giving up my one love of dressing up and dolling up, just to make him satisfied with myself which I failed miserably each time.

After appreciating the beauty around and pigging out fries fishes we went for Daala ride that would take us to the entire round of waterfall, it was like a round boat made of bamboo shoots and looked extremely dangerous, there were few of them discussing about the movie shoot of Raavan, how Abhishek Bachan had dived into the river from one of the hilltops. Adel poked me from behind, it was my turn to get on the daala boat and my body shivered in pain, my heart pounding, skipping beats, I had read about these boats toppling, accidents took place in this 20 feet deep river but I had no choice. Giving up I sat on one of the corners, Adel sat beside be holding my hand and balancing the weight of my side. I was lean and had grown leaner these days, my face had lost all the charm and it was pale yellow, my eyes went deep in a black hole, I was definitely not beautiful and smile was rare on my face, my once chubby cheeks that left dimples on my left side was no more chubby, it had left the permanent dent of hollowness. While Adel was exactly the opposite, he was gaining weight, looked like a growing man, he was the most talkative guy I have ever seen, his dark bushy hair was dense like the forests of Arizona, dove-like eyes and a sharp nose gave him the look of an average good looking man. He had that charm on his face and a shine in his eyes that I lacked; yes he completed me in every way.

The boatman talked about the incidents, accidents, beauty of the waterfalls and that area while the girls were busy feeling the wind in their hair, tapping water with their hands while holding their boyfriend with the other. I once tried to look at the water behind me, and immediately took it off; I wonder what the unseen held within, the marine life, the plants and the unknowns who never wanted to be known like I did. The ones who never wanted to get evaded and we are just disturbing their life and existence by overcrowding the serene place with our presence. The boat stopped at a small beach like an area where there was the sand hill on one side and a stream on the other side, people were taking a shower under the crack of the rocks where the ice-cold water flowed. All of us just got off the boat immediately and rushed towards the stream, I was the last one to get off the toggling boat. Adel gave his hand and I jumped out of it. They all were ready and by the time I reached to the fringes of the sand dunes they were under the flowing water splashing the cold water on each other. I waded my legs in the water a little and took out as soon as I saw a tiny fish trying to escape the spot. Adel asked me to stay there, looking after the belongings of everyone and wait while everyone took the ice cold shower. I also wanted the same to stay back but our reasons were different here, I did not want to go in the water because I was in fear, Adel did not want me to go in the water because my dress would get wet and that would be inappropriate for all the male around, while he took off his shirt and was splashing water and screaming with excitement on each other. I liked when they left me in peace, I felt contented in my space rather fighting hard to fit in.

I was watching them from a distant and it was lovely, everyone laughing and enjoying the gifts of our lord, the nature in the pristine form. As I was striving to enjoy the nature, I started feeling dizzy, I tried to recall what did I eat that would make me feel this, the objects in my vicinity started to drift away, they turned smaller and smaller, my entire body shivering like a drilling machine would do to the earth. I needed help, I panicked and tried to get up to call someone, but failed, I gulped water, held my head and pulled my hair to inflict physical pain but it continued, my thoughts pushed me to the time I have lost her, to deaths and to emergency, to accidents and dreadful phone calls I had received once. I felt my heart had skipped beats and this was the end of another life, another dream, and another saddest story. I collapsed but conscious, I needed help, I screamed without my voice and probably God heard that when I could see someone approaching, it was Lakshita Di, (Neel's sister), she was a kind-hearted woman, she always tried to understand every one of us and being the eldest of all, guided us in our complex matters. She lifted my drooping head and I grabbed her with all my might still shivering helplessly, she sprinkled water on my face, and I opened my eyes. By the time Adel was there too, he was worried, I could read his face, it was the same as on every other episode it had been. I ruined the entire fun of the trip. No one said a word, but my heart knew what a disaster I did to their happy moods and beautiful time, this was why I was never ready to come with them at the first place. They did sympathise with me but who needed sympathy."

I wrote everything that was hurting my heart and by the time it was 4 a.m. I fell asleep on my diary, hoping for the sunshine and another dreadful fight of existence and survival.

— x x x —

Chapter - 2

At Work

It was Ugadi celebration in the office and we were meant to wear something traditional, I remembered my college days when I was the one, the most excited one for these occasions as dressing up was one thing that brought me smile even to my saddest face. Planning, designing, getting ready from head to toe with my girls and hostel nights were the days I just cherished but knew couldn't live it anymore. Adel did not like me wearing such dresses which would seek the unwanted attention of other guys towards me. He was a religious man and wanted the same for me too, I respected his feeling and so his views. The thing he was doing for me would be worth any amount of sacrifice, what if it only cost one tiny source of happiness. He always said happiness is the gift of our lord and we need to please him first in order to be happy and I strictly followed that. Somehow he has allowed me to wear saree on this occasion of Ugadi, by careful vigilance on no skin showing and other essentials. I was happy as this was the first day I would be going to the office with some extra effort on my looks, other days were as normal where I would just sit and file returns, have lunch and come back home in the evening. I hardly knew the names of my colleague as Adel did not like me to interact with any other guy. I had stopped interacting and made a few female friends with whom I could have lunch and take a short break if needed. I was a loyal person, I thought and believed.

It was a royal blue sari with golden border, the blouse of the saree was velvet, high-necked, also covered my entire waist. It was royal indeed, a gift from my father, for the first time in those 10 months, I felt special wearing what I loved and how I loved, I had straightened my hair which was now rough and lacked luster due to hard water of Bengaluru and less of care. My pale skin was covered with a baby like texture from Lakme mousse I applied, darkened my eyes with kohl and wore a choker over the neck of the blouse, I looked good to myself.

Almost running late, I rushed to take an auto for office, Adel was not there to pick me today and that somehow didn't bother me, I was okay to go on my own because had he been there he would have pointed out some flaws in my dress up or make-up or would get mad at me for looking presentable.

I reached office late, as usual, I greeted my boss who was impeccable in time management, he was always there on time, I have never seen that seat vacant, he is there when I come to office and he is there when I leave office, I respected his dedication towards work and responsibility.

He was not liked by many people but he was my favourite, dedicated, always engaged in his work, disciplined and work was all that mattered to him, no politics and no favoritism, unlike other people. I adored him for that reason and for the first time in the history, he complimented me in that sari with a smile on his face, he never smiled, never. People kept complimenting me for the rest of the day; it was a beautiful experience that brought me back to what I was. I felt good, it lifted my depleting confidence because my sad soul needed people around me, who would love me for what I was, appreciate real me and not for what I pretended to be in the case of Adel.

Isn't it a human nature to like appreciation, find happiness in positive strokes from people around us as we are a social being, society plays a role in our personality, recognition works wonders at times, it helps people to become optimistic and hopeful. It drives them to do even better to get more of those remarks.

I hardly had friends now, Adel did not like my interaction with male friends and gradually I had drifted away from each one of them, whereas the rest of my girlfriends got busy with their lives with distance and I was alienated. My best friend, Sukrit was in the same town but I was not allowed to see him either, Adel didn't like him for some reason, he believed a girl and a guy can never be just friends and it would be easy to just stay away as to avoid any complication. I had accepted that too. How could I not, he was everything I had. That day when I returned to meet him in the evening, he looked at me half-heartedly, he didn't like that I had a smile on my face so he just said

"So you did what you like the most"

"I had asked you already, you agreed for that Adel"

"Yes because you wanted to not because I wished"

"But what is the problem with my dress, can't I just wear what makes me happy" I questioned in my frustration. Looking at me irritated, he took my face in his hands and spoke to me in a more understanding way,

"Look, I am just protecting you from all the evil things of the world, and I am protective about you because I love you".

I was too innocent to realise the emotional abuse behind his protective nature and I believed him considering it for my own good. He wanted me to have religious belief and live a pious life and, dressing up, attracting other's interest towards oneself was a sin.

I was more than convinced, maybe I would have done something really bad because of which God is making me suffer, he wanted me to have a love for God but in the process, he just built up my fears against him. He thought he was drawing me closer to God but hardly had he realised he was drifting me far away from all the good things God has to offer. He forgot to remind me that life is to live and not to be suffered; he forgot to tell me that this life was also the gift of that God, where happiness and love were the way to live not fear and worries.

I came back to my paying guest and every word of his, made that huge impact on my mind, I believed that I was wrong all these while and regretted everything I had done in my past, precisely I regretted being happy in my past. Happiness reminds me of the last time I was happy when I was in the second year of my college and that one incident changed my life forever. I didn't want to recall that so I tried to sleep hoping to fix everything, make my life better and these thoughts continued till 2 a.m, it is really difficult to sleep when all you think is why are you not sleeping so I called my mom, I dialed her number but hung immediately after the first ring. I did not want to disturb her this late, she would get worried about me, I never used to tell everything that was going on with me, I always told her about my good work, office, eating schedule and she just cared that, after that tragic incident in family, it had broken her too, she spoke less now. Just then my phone rang and it was my mom, she was probably awake.

"Hello, ammi"

"Ha beta, why are you not sleeping, are you okay"

"Yes I am fine, bas neend nahi aa rhi thi"

"What is it, tell me, is something disturbing"

"No ammi, I was just up watching a movie, but why you are not asleep"

And her voice went down

My mom is the iron woman of my family, she has lived and fought all the toughest battles of her life, she was the single woman bringing up 5 children all by herself, my dad supported financially, he was always away for work and could never get the chance to stay with us. She has served Bhagalpur riot victims, (Bhagalpur–my hometown) helped a number of women in their pregnancy and have always been vocal about the rights and duties of people around. If I start describing her and everything that she is, it would take another separate novel to write about her.

She spoke in a low tone but still firm

"I was trying to sleep, but you must have your office tomorrow, you better sleep"

"Don't worry ammi, I will manage, is everything fine at home, how's the kids doing"

"They are great, Maaz doesn't sleep without me and Mithi is growing up, understanding things better and doing well in studies too."

"I know all that ammi, why are you sounding as if I am talking to you after ages"

"No, what else should I say about them, they are the only hope of my life left"

"Ammi please, don't think about all that, and listen I wore sari today, my friends said I was looking beautiful, I will send you the photographs tomorrow."

I avoided any further conversation and hung up. I didn't want her to remember all that and get even more disturbed. And I slept too.

— x x x —

Chapter - 3

Veer at Office

That day, I reached office early, rather very early and for the first time, my boss was not at his place and none of my team members had come yet. I kept my bag inside the drawer and picked the water bottle to fill, that very moment I saw a sticky note on my desktop, it read "Goodmorning beautiful, have a great day" it was not signed by anyone nor addressed to me so I ignored thinking it might be a note to someone who would have accidently left at my desk. Still, I removed and kept it in my drawer. The very next day, I got the same note at the same place with a cute smile as the signature, then I was sure it was not by accident but someone must have done that on purpose, either to prank me or just for fun. That same note continued for a week, and this time I was sure that this was really something, I had collected all the notes and saved it in my drawer, as they were too cute to be thrown away. I decided to talk about it to my friend with whom I used to have my lunch.

'Sangeet, I have to tell you something'

'Yes tell me, she said carelessly without looking at me as she was busy drooling over her chicken biryani'

'There is someone who keeps sticking notes on my desktop every morning'

'What? Really? She stopped chewing her food, it was the first time I had said something that really interested her and she looked at me with her tiny eyes enlarged'

'And what do those notes read?'

'Nothing much, just morning wishes, smileys, that's it'

'Dude, I don't believe this, you have a secret admirer'

To be honest, I don't believe it either, I would be the last girl anyone would even notice, and besides everyone knows I have a boyfriend, people do notice when he comes to pick me up.'

'What nonsense, just because you have a boyfriend, doesn't mean you are not desirable?'

'Look at me, do I look desirable to you at any angle.'

'Just show me those notes'

'It is in my drawer, you can see'

We finished our lunch and rushed to the ground floor from the tenth floor via glass lift that was the only lift I took, I was too claustrophobic to take closed lifts. She looked at all the six notes and tried to figure out like a detective like she knew each and everybody's handwriting and drawing. She was drawing meanings from each word that was written.

"He is so cool and this is so awesome, don't you feel like knowing the person", she asked amused

"Of course not, I have a boyfriend and Adel is the love of my life, why would I entertain anyone's interest"

"Hello, he is not proposing you, stop zoning every guy as the love interest, what if he just wanted to be friends with you."

"No, a guy and a girl can never be friends and besides Adel will kill me if he hears about all these; I don't want any fight between us"

"Stop talking his words Nuha, don't you have your own interest, liking or opinion whatsoever, she gave me the cold look and left."

I stared at the blank screen, what nonsense was she talking about I thought, of course, I have my interest Adel is my interest and I love him, how will she understand our bond, how will she know our love and attachment that we share. He cares for me, stops me from doing wrong and wants to live his entire life with me. What more do I want? Nothing, I answered to myself and long forgot the notes and secret admirer. That day Adel came to pick me up, it was 7 in the evening, Bengaluru weather does magic by this time of the day and it was breezy, amidst all pollution, the wind managed to be cooler and his scooter got a new mirror that reflected my kohl eyes and I liked myself. He asked about my day and I told everything except the notes episode, it broke me within, there was nothing I hid from him, even if I sneezed more than normal, he knew about it but this was hurting me, not letting him know about it but I knew it would hurt even worst had I have spoken about it to him, his insecurities will surge to another level and he might just behave crazy, it would end up in disaster. I held him from behind and rested my head on his shoulders while he drove me away from the traffic. He liked when I did this, I did it not out of guilt but out of love as he was the only one this close to my heart, always there for me, I came as the first priority in his life and this made me surer of us.

"You look happy today, something special in office"

"No, who said that I am happy because you are there with me"

"My babu, I am always there for you at your worst and your best, in your health and your sickness"

These words, worst, sickness suddenly made me insecure and I held him closer. I will always love you, I said in a softer voice. We had dinner together and he dropped to my paying guest and asked me to sleep right on time. I bid goodbye and that night I slept immediately.

The long weekend had already made me forget everything about the sticky notes and I returned to work. There was no note, my mind explained immediately that either he must be on leave or unwell, I looked around the office floor and by god it was vast, my eyes could not even reach the end of it. My heart sank; as was the one little exciting thing of my day to check what exactly was written in the note, to read it more than once and save it like a souvenir. But at the same time, this thought made me uncomfortable as I thought I might be doing something wrong, why was I even expecting someone's note and brushed away further thought. Same day, I discussed it with Sangeet, over lunch.

"I think he must be on leave, didn't find the note today", I said casually

"What bothers you anyway, you didn't want that"

"Of course, I didn't want it, but I am just saying what if he is unwell or something like that"

"That is none of your concern, but yes, if he is really not in the office so we can easily find out who the person is, I will just look around, as far as I know he must be someone nearby to your cubicle."

"No, you don't have to do anything like that, just ignore all these", I scolded her.

Somewhere in my heart, I didn't want to know who the person was; it was perfect and comfortable in this way, some things are better not revealed.

But the fate has something else in store, the very next day, it was there on my desk, a packet of chocolates and the same note, this time, it was the heights, this exactly was something I didn't want, it was just good with the quotes, I didn't want it to go any step further, it was scary and did disturb me. I immediately went to Sangeet's desk and told her about everything, I gave her the packet of chocolate and left it there. Later in the evening, I received a message on google talk

"Hello, this is Veer, I wanted to talk to you about something"

"I am sorry I don't know you, have we met or is it something work related"

"No, we have not met, I sit three rows behind you and", (three rows behind is where Sangeet sits) I thought.

"And what"

"Just want to talk to you face to face"

"I am too busy with my work, just let me know here itself whatever it is"

"I am sorry but those notes on your desktop"

"Okay so it was you and why did you do this, you know I do not talk to anyone"

"Please don't take me wrong in any way, just meet me once and I will explain."

"Okay 6 p.m in the cafeteria and I signed off"

I never even looked at any guy or thought about it, all my office hour was restricted to work only and lunch time, I hardly took a break for tea or coffee like everybody did on intervals. My desktop was where all my attention was all the time. How can someone still notice me, it was really hard to believe. I am just going to warn him that he better don't do such things anymore or else I might complain this to the HR department,

I sounded like a school girl in my mind but that was the right thing to do.

He came to my desk at 6 p.m. extended his hand for a hello and introduced himself. I said hi blatantly and did not care to give a complete look, but just one quick look had given me his entire picture, he was not so tall, dark, and the boyish built guy, his teeth flashed like the headlight of a motorbike, extremely white and shiny.

"Give me a minute, I will just wrap this and come."

Okay, he replied with a smile and walked ahead, I noticed him this time completely, I must have seen him but not noticed before. I was already late for 10 minutes by the time I finished my work, he must have been waiting for no reason so I took the lift and reached cafeteria. He was there sitting alone on a table with two cups of coffee. Hi, I said again, pretending I have a lot of work and that he needs to hurry up on whatever it is.

"Yes tell me, what you wanted to talk", I talked like a professional

"Where are you from and how long have you been to Bengaluru"

"This is what you wanted to talk to me"

"No, I was just inquisitive"

"But I am not here to answer those questions; you can just come to the point"

"I have been noticing you for a very long time, you do not interact with anyone, go out or don't even come for office get together, don't you like this place or is there something else"

"I don't get time actually, whatever time is left from work, I spend with my boyfriend and it is more than enough. I wanted to tell him that listen dude; I have a boyfriend so if you are thinking any sort of thing, better bug off"

"I know that already, but it is just that you should be more engaged with people around and not stay so quiet and aloof. It would help in your own growth and just because you have a boyfriend, doesn't mean you can't have friends. You don't smile often and staying happy is the only thing we really work for in our life, it is the most important thing."

I just stared at him as he spoke, had he been reading my heart all these time of stalking, did he guess what my mind was into every day. He offered me coffee and I denied, "I am allergic to coffee, I can't."

"I am not bothering you to make you uncomfortable, it's just that I think you are a wonderful person and you need to stay happy, open up a little, there is nothing wrong being happy and you know happy girls are prettier. No doubt you are pretty than any girl I have ever seen."

"Stop, I am sorry I am perfect in my space and need not anyone's sympathy or concerns so please do not keep any notes or chocolates of any sort further. Also being happy or unhappy is my personal choice, you cannot read other's story just by observation so stay away."

And I left the table before he could say anything, it had brought water to my eyes, hint of a tear, Adel says I am a girl who just cries on everything, crying has become my nature so I tried hard to stop it and gulped it down my throat. How could I tell him, I wanted people around me too, I wanted love and attention like every 21 years old girl would want? I wanted to have fun, make stories and fly high in the free spirit. But it was all buried within, layered under my depression and caring boyfriend. It was like a fight with myself, things I could not do because of my depression issue, because of panic attacks and things that I could do was not allowed to do by my boyfriend, I was controlled and my disability just entangled me even more in that relationship, it never allowed me to break free.

Two months passed by, Veer did not give up on me, he had constantly made efforts to talk to me, and fate brought me to the same team, even if I had to ignore I couldn't, we interacted for work purpose only. But somehow he had brought that impact in my life, positive impact, I smiled more and felt good about having someone around me who likes me for what I was and tries to see the good in me. I was chaos within and he knew about it, this had made me comfortable in his company. He would often help me in my work as he was senior to me and much more knowledgeable, taxes can be really complicated and mess up with your brain. He used to ask me to accompany for tea breaks whenever he took one and I still denied but with a smile. Things were good, I was not guilty anymore because he was one of my team members where I strictly talked about work and above all, he knew about Adel, I had convinced myself that there is nothing wrong in the little interaction that we have.

It was a Friday evening, Adel picked me from office and we were supposed to go for Neel's birthday celebration at his place, everyone's coming and shall stay overnight. I was reluctant to go; nothing bothered me than a bunch of excited people put together. How would I like it when I lacked the same energy they had, I lacked the hyper-positive outlook they possessed. And more important I was too ashamed after that Hogenakkal trip, didn't want to ruin his birthday.

"Please don't take me there, I don't like to be among so many people" (well people who don't probably understand me or my problem), I pleaded Adel.

"Why are you a diva, why do you have to create nuisance every time whenever there is something good I want to do, you ruin it all, why can't you be normal enough to enjoy all these and just be fine."

Only if he could realise, it was not that I was a diva, I was sick mentally that no one could see it since it is not physical and hence not visible. I chose not to speak further because my heart cried every time he called me abnormal, I felt miserable, like no one could hate oneself for being what they are, he made me feel how worthless I can be, I wanted him to be happy with me, I know it was not possible with the kind of behaviour I had, I had stopped going to movies, any trip, hanging out with his friends, there was nothing I was doing to make him happy, nothing that a normal girlfriend would do for her boyfriend. So, I quietly sat behind his scooter and he drove off to Neel's place.

I liked the guy Neel was, he was the only among the group with an artistic bend, he had given up his engineering job to take up theater and was doing pretty good. His girlfriend Kaavya was from Karnataka and she was a darling too, she was dusky, fairly built with the prettiest smile. She was a powerhouse of energy, enough to illuminate a house, no wonder Neel fell for her in no time.

Adel and I was already late as everyone had arrived and as we entered, Adel went straight away towards Neel and both of them hugged for a little long. They were childhood best of friends, and I have seen them together always, right from the school days. I wished him too and took my corner seat with a faint hello to everyone. Panda was trying to burn the charcoal of hookah while Zoya helped him. Zoya was a pretty girl with a good fashion sense and a head strong attitude, there were times she has gone dangerously closer to Adel too and to my surprise, he never objected that, had it been some guy that close to me, he would have made me miserable.

I liked to observe from distance and not get involved because I didn't smoke or drink, Adel also never touched alcohol but used to do weeds. They would occasionally drag me into some conversation and I would answer in a low tone that helped me to pull myself out of it and lost in no existence mode. That night every one of them got drunk and danced till they dropped. Some vomited, some got busy with their partners, and some made out publicly. All of these made me sick, it was still 10 on the clock, I checked my phone and suddenly was reminded of my office desk, I doubted that may be I forgot to lock my drawer and it was a non-compliance if the guards finds it unlocked. Veer usually stay late at the office and I thought to message him and ask because calling him when Adel is around is like committing suicide. So I dropped a text message.

"Please check if my drawer is locked, if not please lock it and keep the keys- Nuha"

It was delivered immediately, Adel was beside me and I was scared, what If he checks my phone right at that moment. I felt like I was wrong even though I was clearly not. My phone beeped after five minutes,

And fear gripped me because it drew Adel's attention and he asked

"Who is messaging you this late?"

"No one, I guess service message", I lied

"Give me your mobile", he demanded

"Why do you have to do this in public, you can check this later"

"And he snatched it away; I was frightened as if my life is at stake as if this is the end of the world."

"What the hell, who the hell is this Veer and why is he messaging you at this time?"

"He is my senior in my team, I messaged him to lock my drawer"

"So this is what you are doing these days, this is what keeps you busy at work so you don't even text me from work these days, so how long is it going between you two"

"Please, Adel, there is nothing going, don't you trust me this much, we just have work related talk. And I messaged him today because it was important"

"So you had his number too, what does this mean"

"It is obvious I will have my colleague's number, he is my team member, and don't you have numbers of people with whom you work?"

"Please come inside, I want to talk to you"

While everyone was in their half senses I followed him to Abhi's room, no one was there and he pushed the door behind me.

"Tell me why did you hide it from me, you said you don't talk to anyone in the office"

"What is there to hide about it, and it is not that I am going around with him, I just messaged to ask about my drawer, he is the one who stays back late?"

He screamed at the top of his voice, "what kind of girl are you, you certainly don't deserve to be my wife when you hide such things and talk to guys and don't even let me know"

"What is wrong with you Adel, don't you understand one little thing, I talked to him because it was important or else why the hell would I message him being with you", I screamed too, and it surprised me, I was screaming at Adel, this was the first time I ever did. I did not know what made me that courageous to do so. Maybe the fact that I was not wrong or the recent belief that I had developed in myself or was it

Veer's reinforcement to my mind that I was as good as anyone can be.

He grabbed my chin pressing hard with his thumb, and yelled on my face–"how dare you screamed at me after doing all this wrong and pushed me against the wall" I was shattered once again, my jaw ached and my head started hurting badly. I held my head with both my hands and dropped on the floor like my world once collapsed. The inside of my brain hurt and tears rolled down my cheeks. I had given up once again.

He must have realised so he immediately held me close in his arms, he was in tears too, apologising profusely for what he did. When my sobbing stopped, I pushed him away and asked to leave me. I didn't want him in my life anymore, I wanted to rather get lost than to be with someone like him in such a way. I definitely understood the cycle of abuse now and I realised it cannot be love. Love can never go wrong.

"Please let me go home, I don't want to stay here anymore, I want to go back to my sister.", I cried

I dialed my sister's number and started crying over the call,

"What happened, why are you crying", she got worried

"I want to come to you"; I spoke in broken words trying to stop my sobs

"Yes you can, but tell me what is the matter, is Adel around let me speak to him"

He took the phone and explained that I was just upset on something and that everything is fine, need not worry about.

Falak knew my depression problem, she got convinced to what Adel explained as he was the one pretending to understand me the best. Even though he apologised, asked sorry and begged not to leave him in any condition, my heart was smashed and was not ready to be fixed with any amount of good things. Later that night, I had an extreme headache which led to anxiety because I was worried that something very bad has happened to my head which is the reason I am suffering from unbearable pain. I was rushed to the hospital once again in the middle of the night, it was just Adel and I, rest of them were not in their senses to even know something had happened.

We reached emergency ward of Fortis Hospital of Bannerghatta Road. It was the same hospital I had come earlier to see a psychiatrist for my anxiety issue and they have prescribed me anti-depressants and a mild sleeping pill which I took initially but later had given up. I never understood the concept of anti-depressants, they are the chemicals that are forcing the body to produce happy hormones, I am a human being, and happiness is the way of life, why do I need an external stimulant to do what my body is capable of doing in its natural form. Depression was the social issue not the biological, no one understood that, my social life needed to be fixed first, and chemical composition in the brain would follow next. I always wanted people to understand this.

I was admitted to the emergency ward, I lied on the bed and shivered in the ice cold temperature, Adel held my hand and I held his with all my might, hospitals frightened me always, it brought back the memories that I was running away from, suddenly I could hear the ambulance siren from a distant, I looked at Adel with my teary eyes, "nothing has happened" he assured. I started reading dua in my mind, that had become involuntary by now, as soon as I heard the siren I would just pray for the one who is inside that, it gave me assurance and helped me overcome the negative thoughts because I believed that since I have prayed for the one, I have transferred the worries to my God and he will take the best care of that person. He knows the best, and does the best for every one of us, though my mind confronted often, that if God really does the best for us, why is there sufferings and pain in the world, why couldn't' world run without these. And my left side of the brain ached severely giving jitters to my body, Adel called the nurse and she took my temperature, blood pressure, and gave me a pain killer as the first aid. After the customary treatment, doctor came and read my case; he asked me a few questions about what I do, where I live, my job, work pressure.

"So I think you take your job really very serious, easy girl, you are just a kiddo", doctor smiled at me.

"No, I love my job, it is just that sometimes."

Please follow me, he commanded in sign language towards Adel.

How rude the doctor was, i thought, I was trying to explain things, and he just cut me in the middle and walked off. Of course, he would, I was not the only patient out here and my explanation wouldn't add any prescription. The nurse asked me to rest for some time while she took out the IV and injected it on my wrist hanging a bottle of glucose dripping with the speed of a snail. Adel came to me after his meeting with the doctor and I asked him inquisitively about the matter, like finally getting to know the suspense or the climax of the interesting movie.

"Nothing has happened to you, it is all in your brain and your diet needs to get better."

Every doctor says the same thing but it was a relief that nothing has happened to me; I thanked God in my mind.

"It is just that you need to avoid triggers; migraine attacks are painful and stop taking stress, please", he added.

"A migraine attack, I was once told by a doctor previously but they just doubted it might be, so maybe it is."

"Triggers are extreme sunlight, stress, loud noise and hunger so stay careful, Nuha why don't you understand little things, why can't you just take care of yourself."

"Adel, don't I try to be good, I give my best to stay fit and less of nuisance; I know it is difficult for you to go through all these, taking care of me in such a way but I will give my more than cent percent. Just be there with me."

He held my hand in his and asked sorry for the night as he knew it was him, hurting me such a way and my headache coincided with the episode that just made him feel worst. I forgave him immediately, forgot everything he was doing with me a few hours ago, how could I not, he was there for me even now, sacrificing his peace and worrying about my well-being but in his own way.

I was feeling much better and the bottle had dropped 80% of its content, I wanted to get up and sit, Adel helped me with my needle injected hand and I sat down waiting for the drip to finish. Just then there was some commotion near the entrance, a patient was dragged on the stretcher in a hurry, all the nurses and doctor suddenly got alarmed and made way to the bed by my side. A very giant built doctor arrived, checked the patient who appeared to be a college boy, the doctor was sweating, get the IV nurse, shouted some medicines name, a nurse rushed to get the injections, the boy was now vomiting out blood, he was unconscious.

"Doctor screamed his name,

Rohan, are you with me

Rohan open your eyes

Rohan be with me

What is happening with you?

Rohan can you see me

I am a doctor, can you see me, tell me how are you feeling

Open your eyes, speak, Oxygen Oxygen get the oxygen" the doctors continued to shout in unison.

And the boy could hardly breathe, made continuous painful sound and the doctor screamed again–Get to the ICU now.

And that was all I could remember, I saw Adel drawing my curtains, reading duas to me, and I remembered nothing, I had lost conscious after knowing and being in what that stranger Rohan was into. It had hurt me in my heart and I suffered a complete blackout.

I opened my eyes to find myself in the private ward of patients. A nurse was holding blue colour pill on her palm and was standing by my side waiting for me to wake up completely. Where am I? and what happened to Rohan. Where is he?

Okay take these pill immediately, I will send Rohan in, said nurse.

What, I asked in my mind, why would she call Rohan for me, he doesn't know me and did he just recover overnight, while I was still figuring out, I saw Adel coming towards me.

"How are you feeling Nuha?"

"Did the nurse send you in?"

"Yes she said, you were asking for me"

"No, wait, why am I here, we were supposed to go home last night after the drip, and why are you here, did you not sleep last night, and who changed me into these clothes."

"Nuha, you fell unconscious after whatever happened last night and the doctors advised to admit you here, I thought it would be better if you get few more tests staying here"

"What about Rohan? Is he good?"

"Who is Rohan"

"That guy beside my bed"

"Oh yes, I hope he would be doing fine, he was taken to ICU"

"You hope? Don't you know?"

"I will find out and tell you"

"Adel, please tell them to save him", I pleaded him with tears in my eyes, I was aware it is not Adel who could do anything, but who else do I ask who would reply me immediately, assure me immediately, it was just Adel.

"Of Course Nuha, it must be some drug overdose or something, by now the doctors would have controlled, I am sure he would be doing better."

And my tears turned to sobs and then heavy sobbing, Adel hugged me and to lighten the situation no he said with a smile, "by the way I changed your clothes"

"No, you didn't", I disagreed.

"Yes I did"

"Why would you"

"Because the nurses were too lazy and unwilling to do so, and I was more than willing."

"Oh, I don't believe you"; I was too shy to accept that even though I knew he did that, sometimes I really felt I was blessed to have him, like an angel of life.

"So should I start spotting moles in your secret places"

"No way just shut up" and I hid deeper in the pillow when the nurse knocked, the doctor is on a visit and I got up to let him know I was perfectly okay and would like to take off.

"How are you this morning, with a wide smile on his face, why didn't you tell me last night that you were under a psychiatrist prescription" Doctor asked.

"I was but I had stopped taking those medicines, didn't want to take those"

"Why so, there is always a solution, if not that you should have consulted a psychologist, to undergo therapies, see I am not meaning you are sick, or you have any problem but why not fix something when you still can. I have prescribed some regular tests and you can check out tomorrow morning"

"Tomorrow? But I am fine"

"Yes, you are, there are tests and you are under observation", doctor explained

And the young handsome doctor left the room; I could hear his fading conversation with nurse, and I heard CTscan

"Adel whatever it is, I will not undergo CTscan", I cried to Adel.

"Who is asking you to, and even if you have to it is just a test, not a surgery that you are scared of."

"Adel, I am not feeling good here, I don't like hospitals and tests, and blood and drips and nurses and doctors"

"Oh, enough Nuha, I don't believe you are 21 years old, you are a woman and still behave like a kid, when you will grow up"

I looked at him with my baby eyes, and he came closer, sat by my side on the bed.

Don't sit here, nurses has asked not to, pull that chair and he just ignored everything I was saying, pulled me closer and his eyes were right on my swollen face , I knew those eyes, dark thick lashes, ready to adore me even when I was this pathetic, stinking dettol and medicines. He held my cheeks with both his hands, I closed my eyes, submitting myself as if he owns me, carefully and slowly he kissed my forehead. I opened my eyes, he was smiling and pretended he would kiss my lips but he did not. I liked him that moment even more and respected him. He wanted me for real as his lifelong partner, and for me, I was not in that state of mind to survive any romantic involvement, my mind was already cluttered with fears and anxiety, OCD and panic attacks. So I was satisfied by everything the way it was at that point of time.

I asked him to go home and freshen while I take a quick nap and then we can go for the tests, he asked me to sleep while he waited there by my side, watching me, he knew even when I am asking him to go, I have that fear in my heart of being alone, he knew I was in no position to handle being left alone. After an hour, nurses came in and asked me to follow her to the pathology department for the test, I chose to walk rather being dragged on a wheelchair as I was perfectly fine and could manage that.

They pumped out a tube of blood from my veins and I was okay, the needle did not hurt me anymore, after which they asked us to go to the radiology department. This freaked me out, I pleaded Adel not to take me there, I have seen in movies how they put you in a cave-like structure and leave you all alone in that place.

"Adel, please, I won't be able to breathe in there, my heart starts beating fast even with the thought of it"

"Nothing of that sort will happen and am I not there with you"

"No you don't understand they will ask me to close my eyes and it will be dark and that cave looks like a person is dead"

"It is really scary Adel, please let's not go there", he was already talking to the nurse of the radiology department, he offered me a glass of water and I gulped it in a go.

"Please, Adel", by now my eyes were dripping all the bottles of glucose they had injected in me. And he did not listen to me, just kept holding my hand.

They made me lie on that narrow bed which had a slider in it, that would slide under the radioactive machine and know all about what my brain holds in.

I was still crying and my heartbeat was racing, I held Adel's hand tightly and was not ready to leave.

Nurses asked me to leave his hand as it had to be rested on my chest, Adel assured me he will be there right by my side, watching me and promised nothing would happen and slowly I left lose his hand.

It was like hell, going into something that made me feel suffocated, breathless not because it was that uncomfortable but because it was all in my mind. Those few seconds of torture drained all my energy and life out of my body. When I was slid out of the machine, I opened my eyes and found no one in the room. Got up to see Adel was behind the see through glass watching me with a smile, I wondered how did he manage to maintain that smile in spite of all these commotion and chaos I create all the time. Later he took me out and said it was not allowed for normal people to stay there as the radioactive wave affects us and may harm.

"So the nurses lied to me", I asked like a child

"Yes, you were acting so weird, even children don't, they had to assure you."

And I hung my head in shame thinking children don't fear death as I do.

— x x x —

Chapter - 4

Confession to the Psychologist

As suggested by the doctor, I had to see the psychologist today, who would not ask me to swallow pills but would make me feel better with his therapies and other procedure. I was convinced to these as may be practicing something would make someone feel better as that is how we fell in the trap of causes too. Incidents, some accidents, moments make us so vulnerable that instills lifelong fear in our nerves so we fall prey to the maladies of mental health, similarly what if some therapy, some tasks would just undo all those. It convinced me more than that forced serotonin and dopamine which was artificially created with no guarantee of its perpetual existence.

Adel could not accompany me today, had it been just work he would have taken off but his father was in the city for the visit so he had to tap closer to him. This was the first time I would go to a doctor without his company, although he kept texting continuously on my mobile and I was giving him all the reports of my whereabouts.

I waited outside the psychologist cabin, a line of chairs were arranged just outside his cabin wall and it was all vacant, unlike other physicians and neurologists where the place was bustling with patients. I wondered if I am one among the handful who suffers from depression and mental health issues or are there many people and they don't turn upto medication or therapies. But I don't see more people around like me, who get anxious on every little thing that I do, who worries, panic and overuse hand sanitisers. With this I remembered the auto that I took to the hospital, I took out my sanitiser to sanitise my hands and I did that till my wrists. Who does that generally, nobody fear a normal staircase, but when I look at round twirling stairs in my paying guest, the first thing that comes to my mind is if I slip I will definitely break my spine, my head might bang on one of the iron rods or break my bones. Or who fears to be alone, what if I am all by myself and I get a panic attack, and then who would be there to support me, tell me that everything is fine, who would rub my hands and feet to get my blood running. That way I could lose my life, that fragile life is, everything shall end. See who thinks this much, no one I exclaimed to myself. But what if many do have these fears or suffer such a way but they don't let anyone know in general like I don't discuss these things to anyone except Adel. Whatever it is, people need not be ashamed of what they are, I thought. I was sad about what I have become but not ashamed about it. My disability to do normal of things made me sad, inability to make Adel happy made me sad and when he has to undergo unnecessary chaos because of me, it made me sad.

My never ending thought was interrupted by the call bell and a nurse gave me a slip kind of getting in the cabin, his door read Dr. Adarsh, which is a very uncommon name in South India. And immediately I thought he is one among the 13.5k psychiatrist/psychologist in India with a population of about 1.2 billion, referring to the article I read recently.

Good morning Doctor, I bowed before him just like my school days, it was certainly the lifelong gift of the convent school, Excellence, Virtue and Discipline was the motto of my school, and discipline was something instilled in our blood, every

Josephites I would say, (Josephites–all the kids from St Joseph's School, located in the heart of a small town, Bhagalpur).

"Sit down young lady, what brings you here", he asked in his kind tone.

He was a mid-aged man in his late forty's, with the charm of a young energetic man, his spectacles rested on the bone of his nose as if piercing his intellectual eyes into my mind reading it all. His year's old experience was visible on the lines of his foreheads and his crooked smile was both friendly and like a mystery.

I searched for things to start the conversation and my mouth got dried, of course, I wouldn't have told him about my problems right away, what brings me there would be no different than what brings each single patient to him. So I rather chose to answer in a more secure way, I was referred to you by Dr. Sharma, he had said it would be good if I consult you, I have been previously under psychiatrist who advised me medication but I stopped taking those.

"I didn't want to take medicines to solve some problems that are in my perception, thoughts and something which I know I can change", I gave my reasons even before he asked for it.

"You already have the solution to your problem dear; tell me what you do"

"I work as a tax professional"

"So lot of number crunching job, does that bother you"

"No, I love my job, I like working"

"What else do you like?"

"I like writing, reading, and painting"

"What do you write", he continued questioning

"I write whatever I observe, experience or fantasise about"

"Do you write how you feel"

"Yes, I write that in my journal, it feels like I have spoken to someone, sharing everything with the journal makes me feel light."

"Where is your family, who all are there in your family"

"My dad lives in Mumbai, he had always been there for his business is set up in Mumbai, my mom is in Bhagalpur, Bihar, she never liked any other place than her own home, we are five siblings. Falak is an automobile engineer working in Mumbai, my two brothers stay with my mom and I work here"

"And what about the other one, you said five right"

"Who Sarah", I exclaimed as if he knew everyone by name

"She is good"

"You have a beautiful family and I understand, they are all dispersed, catering the demands of this generation. What bothers me, why don't you seem comfortable, is there something you want to tell"

"I fear, fear from everything you can imagine about, I feel like life is so flimsy, it can be broken at any moment, and things can change forever at any point in time. It can leave you devastated and still demands to live, to behave normal, to think usual, to come up to all the expectations. No one then addresses that trauma, no one cares what is inside your head, what are you going through, all they care about is how well are you fitting in the system, how well you behave socially, how well you cope up with your personal life."

"But that is what life is all about, don't you think you worry a little too much"

"Little? I worry a lot, I was worried sitting outside your cabin, I was worried while traveling from my home here, I worry every second of everything that is happening and I have no control over that. Nothing makes me happy, nothing excites me, I have stopped dreaming, stopped aiming, stopped planning, living a day carefully is all I can think about, that is all I can afford to."

"Do you have friends or someone close"

"Yes I have a loving and the most caring boyfriend"

"Do you love him equally?"

It hit me like a boulder, I loved him yes I loved him, what was I thinking, I should have answered him right away, that is why I am with him, and my mind over flooded with opinions on something so obvious, it screamed, 'tell him that you love him, do you really love him or is it your fear holding him close, do you really want him after all that he stops you from, after all the worst treatment he gives, do you really have that true affection without any need, any fear.'

"Nuha, I asked you something", doctor poked me with his question.

"Yes, yes doctor, I do love him, he has brought me to the right path, right direction of my life, he has patience with me, he adores me when I don't feel good, he goes out of his ways to make me feel comfortable, and he is also usually happy with me as long as I behave the way he wants me to."

"Well, tell me about your past life, any incident or any accident."

"My past life, I was not like what I am now, I was a cheerful girl who did not care about anything, who did not fear anyone or any calamity, I was the strongest one of my family, I had friends, I had enemies and I lived recklessly and enjoyed every bit of my life, most importantly I was fearless."

"What changed you to this paranoid?"

"I am not changed doctor, I am being myself, I wanted to escape, I wanted to run away from all that, I was praying to god on my knees, begging for day and night but he chose to change me, he changed me, I didn't change myself, I didn't and I broke in tears, I was sobbing heavily, the doctor called the nurse and she gave me tissues and held my hands, she asked me to stay calm and the doctor kept on saying"

"Relax Nuha, there is nothing to worry about, the past should not hold this much of importance in your life, look at me, see if you are not feeling okay we can continue this later, just relax"

"If you want, since you said you can write down what you feel would you be able to write me the account of everything that you wanted to tell me today especially your past."

I controlled my sobs and replied with regained courage "yes I can do that", he gave me the prescription with no medicine but just his e-mail id.

"Have a good day and write me soon after that I can call you for another visit, and remember what you said to me in the beginning you can control everything, rationalise things, it is all in your mind. Your mind is in your body, you are the supreme being of the God's beautiful creation. Remember what you believe in. And yes don't forget that Nuha itself means intellect."

"Thank you, doctor", and with a bunch of tissues I left his room, I walked home and took a long sleep. The whole time Adel kept on ringing my phone, I was fast asleep so could not answer his call. When I woke up, I was frightened at the number of calls he had tried, I called him back immediately justifying my sleep and how I forgot to update him. He hung up getting mad at me, this did not bother me today, I was too occupied with the thoughts of my recovery and what in the world should I do to bring back me, the old me.

I stared the doctor's e-mail id and decided to write

Dear Doctor,

It was the last night's annual fest hangover that was not allowing me to get off my bed and answer my phone kept at an arm's distance. It is always the happiness code that allows you to dress up and show up, girl's favourite right to do. I was no less a girl. And it rang for the third time, I pulled myself to reach to the phone and it was something unusual, why would my mamu call up early in the morning, for god's sake he never ever calls let alone the morning. I answered already awake

Are you still sleeping beta?

Yes mamu, Assalamualaikum, kaise hain?

I am good, okay I called you to inform that there is nothing to worry about, but Sarah has met with an accident and there are little burns.

Burns, accident, what is it, my head was spinning, I don't know what hormones were released from my body, it made me shiver, shiver like in terror, something that has gripped on me and I was unable to comprehend anything further, I dropped my phone and fell back on my bed. That was the first time I had felt a fear so frightening. Fear of the worst, of unimaginable and suddenly my mind becomes uncontrollably disturbed, I regained myself thinking nothing bad would happen, it might be a minor accident, so all I need is to visit home, things will be fine as it had always been. As mom tells that to everyone, problems are there to test us and then things fall back to the place and it always ends up happy.

I tried calling my mom, it rang full for the first and then again, no response, I tried to my father and same no response, that had made me more paranoid. While I was thinking what to do next, my sister, Falak called up and asked to pack a small bag as we have the flight in two hours. Airport was nearer to my place so I packed my bag in a hurry, took bare essentials and was waiting for her to pick me up.

What is so urgent that everybody seems to be worried and is it this urgent that we need to take a flight to Patna, as there is no airport in Bhagalpur, so we cannot fly directly all these running in my mind; we needed to take the train from Patna to Bhagalpur later. There was a knock at my door, the security guard of my hostel had come to pick my small bag and informed my sister was waiting downstairs, I denied his offer to help and walked the stairs, I could see Falak from a distance and I can tell you she was not fine, anxious and taking a sip of water every minute as if hit by the Sharan desert wind. She hurriedly hugged me, we do not do that on our usual meetings, it freaked me out and I assured her that mamu had told me it is a minor accident and slight burn.

"Don't worry na, she will be fine, by the time we will reach there, she will be all fine and teasing us of our stupidity as she always does. We can then go for her homemade beauty mask and enjoy this spring together." I forced a smile but she did not care. Anyways I tagged along and we reached the airport in half an hour, throughout the taxi time, she did not speak a word, rather fidgeted, looking at her black phone screen and other times staring outside the window glass. I was a positive person, I feared the worst at first but the reassuring words of my mamu echoed my ears and that gave me immense confidence in my optimism. My mom has made me believe that as long as we are good and do good, nothing bad can happen to us. Nothing worst can touch us as our guardian angel is always with us protecting in return to our good deeds. And Sarah was the gem of a person, she has never ever broken a tiny piece of anyone's heart, didn't utter a bad word for someone or I guarantee you she wouldn't even have answered back to a hurtful comment, cursed anyone even if the person would have stolen her precious treasure. And how do I define her character and her beauty, her face was the exact mirror of what was inside, her divine looks gave the angelic persona? We never looked like her sisters as she was insanely beautiful and we were like her step sisters.

Sarah was the carbon copy of my mom and believe me my mom was the epitome of beauty as a girl. My dad was so thrilled of her beauty that he used to call her Madhubala. Her waist long black and thick hair added a streak of angelic charm to her small round shaped face with a perfectly aligned nose and a frail tiny pair of lips. Her doe eye held charcoal black pupil that would make anyone stare a little longer, it still reflected energy and hope in its most divine form. So was my eldest sister, Sarah. Sarah got married at the tender age of nineteen and she had two children, a girl and a boy in her 5 years long marriage. It was arranged by my parents, of course, she did not get enough time to understand her own likes and dislikes before she could analyse herself what would she have desired for, she was already tied to a man much older to her. I never approved of her marriage, but I was too young to make a difference in major decisions at that moment of time.

After the check in, we were waiting for our boarding time, while Falak still seemed in a deep shock, I asked if she would like to eat something and she denied with a nod. I didn't want it either and so I chose to observe things around rather pushing myself to the thoughts of worst possibilities. There was a long line of army people boarding a plane to Srinagar, probably off on their duty. Who likes to leave their loved ones and go to a place where there is no guarantee of lives, unsure of the fact if they could ever return to find them back? Their heads were held high, eyes were dry but I can tell you they had a drooping heart, sagging legs with every step they took. If only someone could stop them to stay with their loved ones forever and never have to leave them. But the love of their duty towards the country and people like us, made them head forward and maybe that was the motivation behind all the sacrifice.

We boarded our plane, and after this journey, I would ask you never to board this airline ever, I am letting you now because I can't wait to tell you this. Flying crews are not so hospitable, one thing that they are specialised in; food is awful, not because airline food is such but because that was actually worst. And the engine sounds like a blocked exhaust of your kitchen or old age dad's scooter in the times of Nana Patekar. In the middle of the flight, the captain announced: "we are 35000ft above the ground, the temperature outside is chilling -40 degree, the weather is cloudy and we might find turbulence as we approach Patna airport". I don't understand the significance of this announcement, are they gonna give us a thrill of such adventure or freaking us out of the fact. Well, depend on the receiver's end. We had our food and by the time we approached Patna, we faced a number of jolts and dark clouds surrounded us. There was a time when the jolt was so severe that a few of the co-passengers freaked out in fear, and the captain kept the announcement live requesting not to panic as the jolts are due to weather disturbances and there is nothing to worry about. But I have watched it in movies how the captains keep on announcing positive even when both the wings of the plane is on fire, they still ask not to panic when the plane is about to crash in the middle of the ocean. I was strong with my mind, I played my mind well and often restored at such times of crisis. I held Falak's hand to calm her down a little and after a few minutes the plane regained and there was a surge of smiles on the faces of children and elderly. I was back in confidence once again. The plane landed safely and the flying crew stood at the door thanking us and we faking thank you with a forced smile.

As soon as we reached the taxi stand, it started raining heavily, the clouds were hell black and the noon time looked like midnight. Heavy thunder and lightning brought gloominess all around like an apocalypse. This was the time that really frightened me, I usually enjoy rain and such weather, but it was the beginning of February, what made the sky cry, the negativity tried to grip on me once again and this time it did not leave. I called up mom and still no response, called my brother and he disconnected too. Why are no one worried about us, we have been traveling and it was so not like how they behave when we travel all by ourselves. No one was asking us about our whereabouts and why even mamu not calling us again. After a while someone called and I answered the call but Falak grabbed the phone instantly, she said ha we are here in Patna, will be boarding the train in an hour.

That's all? I asked, you should have at least enquired why no one is answering our calls, if everything was okay and she said in a raw tone,

"it's all going to be fine"

Going to, is it not fine now, what can be so wrong,

I told you it is just a meager fire accident, it happens all the time, you also know how Sarah is so much into cooking.

Yes, I thought, I know how delicious she cooks. She is specialised in Biryani, mouth watering aloo mutton Kolkata style Biryani since she had spent a significant number of years in Kolkata with Amma (grandmother) she knows all the Bengali delicacies. All my friends devoured her recipes; I remember when I had invited my friends and my crazy gang over dinner.

Sarah cooked Kolkata Biryani and Meetha pulao for that night, spicy curd drink being obvious along with her special Biryani. It was one eventful day because that morning itself I had my first period and I had screamed from my washroom, about to faint with stupid thoughts of unknown disease occupied my brain. She had come running to my rescue and when I had narrated and showed the splat of blood all around, she just smiled and said, "kuch nahi hua hai", what? I had screamed back, I am bleeding like a chocolate fountain, non-stop, and you are saying, nothing happened.

She then had came back with sanitary napkin and asked me to stick it to my panty. I did as she asked me to and then I could relate my practical suffering to all the biological theory read in class. I thought it would definitely ruin tonight's dinner. But she was always there by my side to my rescue, I could sense the look my mom gave me and I tried to hide somewhere behind the curtain and never look in her eyes ever again, I have reached puberty. Was it the matter of embarrassment or a good sign of my growth, well whatever I was more concerned about that night and things I have dreamt about on number of nights imagining him being at my home and I would then get enough time to look into his eyes and know what he felt about me, was it the same as I drew pictures in the sky, connecting stars to spell Nitesh or did he even notice me.

We reached Patna Junction and it was really frustrating to find that the train we had planned had been canceled due to heavy downpour and the next train is only after six hours. We were too young and tiny to take care of ourselves at the place like bustling station and you never know when do you get robbed or snatched away of your precious belongings. Though we never wore anything like heavy gold or precious watches, therefore, we wouldn't have grabbed any unwanted attention. We took a corner seat at the platform and rested in our disappointment, I got some chips and cold drinks to keep us hydrated. Just then a vendor passed by repeating in a tone that was so home, "jhaalmuri, jhaalmuri", coming across this, Falak, for the first time of the day asked to buy jhaalmuri, it was her favourite, it is a famous snack of Bihar. While we gulped our cold drinks after hot jhaalmuri, I could recall how Nitesh was not so used to eat hot chilies and was in tears after that dinner. He did not let us know that he was feeling uneasy while he ate all the spicy food at the dinner table, only running for the bathroom after. Sarah was rushing with sugar water and boiled rice to his rescue. I wanted to laugh at him, but his tears made me feel worst and for the first time I could feel, how difficult it is to watch someone you like in trouble, how do people not care about their loved ones, why the neighbour uncle is so violent and abusive to his wife.

I don't know what was love, but even that likeness was so intense that I couldn't see tears in his eyes, that too those tears because of the hot chili. After he settled himself, we had taken a stroll on our terrace and luckily it was the full moon night. Sky was full of twinkling stars and the blue light coloured the entire mango orchard in front of our house. I was wondering what would he speak about, would he know my feelings for him and read everything from my passion dripping eyes. I am generally passionate about everything that I am attached to and that I love, be it my personal diary or a small key ring gifted by him. He looked at me for a while and that made me uncomfortable, "you are pretty" and took his eyes off me. I knew not what should I reply back therefore just smiled. He was then all appreciating about how caring Sarah is and that I am lucky to have a sister like her. That I was definitely, she is one of the charms of our entire family, I thought.

After a while, a man walked to us and enquired about the next train and platform number for the same, I don't understand the Indians, we have a complete information desk dedicated for the enquiry purpose but people are too lazy to take their inquisitive mind to the right places and ends up in wasting more of their time and energy. I pointed towards a big hoarding that was screaming, "enquiry". He gave me a stern look and walked away. It was a long wait of 6 hours, we couldn't even doze off, as it was just two of us, and the place was not so conducive for the idea. After the long wait we finally boarded our train, it was local intercity train which was chair car kind and after sitting idle for 6 hours we couldn't even lie down and take rest. We were exhausted already that as soon as the train started we fell asleep in our sitting posture itself.

I was making mud dolls and utensil while both Falak and Sarah flipped my handmade toys and left me in tears, they laughed like hysteria. I ran to the welcoming embraces of Amma (grandmother), she held me close and reprimanded the other two with a wink. I knew she did not actually scold them but just consoled me. Their laughs echoed my ears, her visual laugh played like a slow motion graphic in my mind and sent chills through my body to which I woke up. It was a sudden brake of the train; someone must have pulled the chain, as the train is running in Bihar, where it is very easy for the local passengers to just pull the chain at their doorstep instead of waiting for their stations to arrive. After a little commotion, the train got its speed running. February is beautiful generally; I could see new sunflower plants in the fields in their full bloom. Rose plantations and marigolds, these are harvested for commercial purposes as these flowers are majorly used in temples and mosques and dargahs. Gradually my eyes closed and don't remember when I fell asleep admiring those endless fields of flowers.

Woke up to the noise of restless passenger hurrying up to get down the train, it was our destination, Bhagalpur. For the very first time in the history of records, no one cared to pick us from the station, therefore, we took a rickshaw to home which is three kilometers from the station. Every time we visit home, it is like a pool of people including, brothers and friends of brothers and uncles and neighbours, already waiting for us at the platform, this was very unusual as no one turned up. We reached tired and blackened with the long journey, though it was not that long but it turned out exhausting because of all the waiting and the journey of local passengers train. We don't have to knock the gate as there is no main gate to the aangan and it is ever welcoming. But today was it weird as we couldn't find anyone in the house, our neighbour grandmother was sitting there idle and we rushed to her asking about what the matter was and where is everybody else. She hugged us and began crying, this was where my heart sank and it was like someone took my heart out of my body, there was something missing in my heart and I was not able to reason anything. I asked in a plain tone, what is the matter to which she said, "sab log hospital gaye hain",

There is only one hospital in the Bhagalpur city and I spent not even a single minute in asking further and rushed to catch a rickshaw to the hospital. Reaching to the hospital, we met our Mamujaan, the one who had called me the previous night. I asked him what had happened, where everybody is, and where is Sarah. He was in tears and I knew, this time, something not good. I screamed at him and said tell me what had happened, instead of screaming back he calmed me and Falak, and when he started saying everything I was listening, I was just listening and picking up lines in the middle, ignoring his irrelevant words and focusing on what my heart was screaming to know. "Last night, Sarah was cooking and then there was a gas cylinder leak and she met with an accident, and some parts of her body got burnt".

Cylinder leak?

Some parts?

Yes, it was an accident, he reassured.

And all we could ask was where she is now, he exclaimed, she was admitted to this hospital but due to inefficient equipments, she has been referred to a burnt specialised hospital in Bokaro.

Inefficient equipment, this was where I knew. It was not a minor burn, it was not a small accident, it was not and my body dropped flat on the ground, accident, burn, inefficient equipments, it echoed my mind and I lost my conscious. It was a blackout and I couldn't stand it. When I opened my eyes, I found myself on the bed of the same hospital, I got up looking for my slippers and all that I could say was, take me to Bokaro, take me to Bokaro. Take me to my sister; take me to her, Sarah. And my mamujaan, my sister, Falak, and a friend Imran accompanied me; they were constantly asking me to calm down.

Calm down at what, my sister was in the hospital, god knows what she would be undergoing, how could I have calmed down, to what should I have calmed down. We took the bus as there was no train at that time, and we were said it would take five hours to reach Bokaro. Five hours, how would I contain my heart in my chest for five long hours? It was Imran who asked me to take a sip of water, while I restored my overwhelming emotion I noticed Falak, who was all the while composed, containing herself in the most silent way. It was the saddest I had ever seen. She was quiet, looking in the oblivion, I cried watching her, she was never like that, she was always strong, here she was tearing herself apart within, not bringing out her fears on her face because she knew it would affect me, I would react and that was definitely bad for me after that blackout. We did not talk a word; Imran would occasionally ask for chips or water and would try to talk over something or the other.

It was 1.00 a.m. there was no sign of any light in between, except the occasional bus or truck crossing ahead of us with high speed. The siren was ominous, believe me, it was ominous, it seemed that dark night had brought the truckload of devils and evils due to which the entire environment has sunken in negativity and gloominess. To my surprise not a single person was smiling, I do not know what the matter was, has everyone's someone has met with an accident, why couldn't I see any happiness around. It might be that when your hurt is sunken in morose, your eyes fail to pick happiness and beauty around. Falak and I did not talk a word, I rested my head on her shoulder and she rested her head back on mine. I knew it had been the entire day, hectic and tiring on flight, train, and rickshaw and now this inter-state bus. I tapped her hand like mother's do to their babies to make them fall asleep and in a few minutes of caressing, she fell asleep on my tilted head. I was in no position to move my head and I remained like that so that her sleep is not disturbed. There was a tornado running within her and that did need a rest for some time. While I was speculating things, what would have gone so wrong that she had to be referred to a specialised hospital, ok it is just burns, she will definitely recover very soon, and then those haunting thoughts of burnt marks crossed my mind, but then I consoled myself saying that, it is okay even if the marks remain it would definitely go with time and even if it remains, that would not distort her beautiful self, her beautiful heart and her beautiful smile. I was certain, she would look as beautiful as ever, and how do I know what if the burn did not reach her face, her face would be completely oaky, I knew it would be completely fine, why should I worry for that. I am just too worried about the pain she might be in. If a small patch of our skin gets burn somehow, the pain is enormous, what pain equals to the burn in that large amount, I had no clue about the measure of that large amount. How I wished it could be as little as it could be.

Time passed, and we reached Bokaro with the first ray of sunlight. I prayed to Allah for the first time that entire period, all I wished was to find her okay, to look at her and hoped everything to fall back as it was. Even the brightest of the morning looked haunting and traumatic."

How I wished I stopped everything here itself, because after this I do not like to write a single word, how could I have lived following that. Writing about it is as painful as living it. I still continued for it was important for my doctor to understand everything that was buried within me.

"Hospital stood on the dusty deserted road, even the dust appeared red, like it's bleeding, spring breeze had left it displaced and the particles suspended in the atmosphere in abundance, more than it was on the ground. It formed misty layer of adulterated air, hard to breathe, hard to breathe for all the traumatic reasons life was pouring.

I saw my mom from a distance, wrapped in a faded brown cotton sari, her hair was in a mess, her face deprived of sleep or rest, looked tattered and broken, her eyes were swollen like she has been crying her eyes out for million years, yet she was there standing tall like she always have.

Oh! What do I tell you about this Woman?

Married at the age of fourteen and mother at sixteen, she has been the magic of many lives ever since. She, the other of five has stood for everything that was right, from her family to the families around she would not stop caring for anyone.

My mom burst in tears as soon as she saw us, she hugged Falak and she too broke out just like her, I didn't cry because I was still very hopeful about my sister, my Sarah. I hurried up towards the ward leaving them behind and what I saw demolished me for life.

I peeked from the private room of the hospital, it read Burn Intensive Unit; there was a bed right in the middle of the room. There she was, lying still, wearing oxygen mask, her body was covered with a raised structure forming a dome. The sheet was white, the dome was white, the walls of the ward were white and her hazy visible face was black and swollen, her feet peeping out of the sheets were skin less under the white bandage. She has suffered 94 per cent of burns on her body, my mom cried from behind holding my shoulder. I turned to her immediately, and sunk my head deep in her chest, I wanted to get lost in there forever and never see the white light again. Falak wanted to get inside and see her, she walked inside regaining courage and keeping up the hope, I looked from a distant; she was hesitant to reach to her bed and with every heavy step she forwarded, she battled hard to breathe, my heart was pounding as to please return to me with hope and only hope.

Sarah was conscious and looked at Falak with the kindest eyes and spoke with her courageous voice, why did you all come this far, should have taken rest at home, I will be fine and be back soon. And I watched Falak breaking in tears and then loud cry, Nurses took her out and my heart broke in pieces. I rushed to the doctor's office and asked about Sarah's condition. And what doctor replied made me cringe; I could have traded anything in the world just to see her okay.

"Generally, this much of burn victims do not survive, but let us have faith on above, God will help."

I rushed outside, running in unison to find God, just to have one single chance to ask her life back, one light of hope to kindle, one prayer of lifetime. Found myself in front of a vast green field, probably the compound of that huge hospital. I dropped myself to the green grass and cried my heart out. I made a deal with my God, I would never ask anything, anything in the world only if this one last prayer is granted. I bribed him with everything I had ever come across, to visit all the holy places, to serve his humanity, to be the best soul of the world, to be obedient and religious and do everything it could take to please him. Just for once, for once he answers my prayers, I kept crying to myself. I kept weeping and weeping till Falak spotted and asked me to come for dinner. Of course no one was in that condition to gulp even a morsel, and still we sat customarily eating. No one talked, no one even dared to look at each other's eyes. No one was allowed to go near to Sarah, as doctors did not allow for the contamination fear. And ask me, I did not dare to go even a bit closer, I did not even see her when she was taken to a different ward on a stretcher, I did not dare, I just could not. How could I have done that, she was the most beautiful girl on earth and with a heart of gold, how could I have seen her in that condition, in that pain, that suffering, it was like my body parts are being chopped away every time I thought about the pain she was in. There was nothing I could do, all I wished was if only I wake up to find everything was just a nightmare, but I never woke up to that. It was reality hitting hard on us, the apocalypse of our family.

Following morning, mamu and mami came to us and asked us to leave, as they will be taking care of everything and assured us thing will be fine, we had no good place to stay there. We denied and insisted to let us stay there, but mom forced us to leave and we were sent back home as we needed to take care of two other angels of our family, Maaz and Mithi, a two years son and five years old daughter of Sarah. They must be missing their Maa and would be struggling with chaos back at home. So we agreed to come back, only to find them miserable and worried. As we entered home, Mithi came running towards us and asked

Maa did not come?

She will be coming soon my baby, just taking a little longer to recover, but see I got chocolates for you

No, I want to go to Maa, I want to see her, please take me there.

I looked at her eyes, it was of Sarah's, her tiny lips and oval shaped face was perfectly aligned as her mother. She will grow up to be exactly her, I thought and tears rolled down my cheeks. I hugged her and couldn't say anything while Falak looked for Maaz who had the saddest eyes a child could ever have. I remember last time when I was home for vacation, I playing with him and every time I acted as if I am hurting his Maa, he would take a cane and run after me screaming all around the house, oh! How happy it was. Today, he was the quietest, generally a child would cry if he wants something, to make his wishes fulfilled, but he was hauntingly silent staring in oblivion. How it broke my heart, everything was breaking me bit by bit and then all of a sudden. Falak and I made them sleep early hoping the next morning would bring hope and it would bring everything at its place. I closed my eyes praying God, "if not for me, please, please God, bring back these angel like kids their mother back. That was the last night of where I kept holding on to hope, prayers and optimism without a sleep on single second.

And right at 6 a.m. the dreadful phone rang, it was my mamujaan on the other side

"We are in the ambulance, coming back with Sarah's body, she is no more beta, and he broke in tears."

Suddenly Sarah a woman, a daughter, a mother, a wife became her body. That ended everything Doctor.

Thanks and Regards

Your mental patient

Nuha

And even today my heart aches,
If only, I would have showed my love a little more
You would have known what importance you hold
If only I would have asked why you sad
If only I would have questioned your worries again and again
If only I would have read your impeding mind
With claws of such doom looming around
You would have never,
Never, taken that end.

— x x x —

Chapter - 5

Break from Office

As my universe was falling apart probably to form another as they explain in String Theory. It validates existence of things before Big Bang, how the Big Bang could have been the collision of two universe or simply falling apart of a universe into another. Whatever it might be, I was unable to collect back my pieces. That was when Adel had supported my universe as a pillar of support.

I woke up being thankful and obliged to everything that has turned my life into, Adel has always encouraged me to stay thankful to God for every little thing and show gratitude and he couldn't be more right. After Sarah, the harsh truth of life had instilled the fact, how fragile the life is; how easily your life can be changed from a perfect fairyland to hell of fire, burning in the struggle to survive.

I had restored my life after the harsh reality had hit me hard, completed my graduation and took a job like everybody else, came into a relationship just like a normal girl but I could not maintain that relationship like a normal girl, because my needs, my insecurities and my fear made me someone else. This relationship turned out to be everything but a romantic relationship. He wanted me in a certain way that I was not; I wanted to be what I was but not brave enough to go against his wishes. He wanted me to stay happy on his terms, I wanted to stay happy on my terms and neither of it could happen. He was white and I was black, he had hopes, I had none, he was patient, I was restless, he was the mountain of my life holding on to the river, who wanted to just flow but stayed and stagnated. All his rules and regulations, expectations and restriction ate away my zest to live and he hardly realised that. I was in distress, unable to stand up on my own; I needed him all the time, that was my medical condition, but he could have let me live, would have showed me the positives of life rather exposing my fears to the worst and imposing things. I don't remember when that love turned into a routine, more of an obligatory feeling. It was more of gratitude, a responsibility, fear, a relationship which lacked the charm of faith, young love, wild and free.

I had to return back to work that day, my boss was very strict but a kind man. It was difficult for me to go back to same routine, same people and not talk to Veer. I was unsure about my response, how would I avoid him and stay away as far as I can. I had to stop talking to him, break all kinds of contact even if those meant nothing, Adel did not like me to stay in touch with anyone, be it for anything. And after all that happened, I looked like a criminal in my eyes and it all appeared valid to me because who was there by my side throughout. It was not Veer who stayed beside my hospital bed sacrificing his sleep and peace of mind, It was Adel and he cared for me, what more did I want.

"Is everything alright? I pinged you, you did not reply". Veer stood right before my desk.

"Yes, all good, I was just busy with work"

"Ok, get it done soon; we shall go for lunch together"

"Ah, Veer, no, I am not hungry today, you go ahead, I will have it later"

"Ok, but you should eat first, we can go for tea in the evening then"

He left after his declaration, it was really difficult to just say no and deny everything all at once, how should I do it, I wondered. It was nothing wrong, he was not doing anything wrong so I did not have any reason to be rude to him and hurt him. I have never been rude to people, not even to people who have actually hurt me. This was a difficult situation, but I needed to do that anyhow, it would be a crime If I did not, I would be wrong in my eyes if I was wrong in Adel's eyes. Yes he was my mirror, I saw myself the way he saw me, I perceived myself the way he did to me, I was judged by the way he judged me, everything was wrong if he said so and everything was right if he believed so.

Sharp at 5.00 p.m. Veer was once again tapping my table for tea and I could just look at him, I kept on staring trying to adjust my pupil from prolonged exposure to screen to his face.

He waved his hand before my eyes and I said "no"

"What, why are you behaving weird today"

"What weird, I am just fine, I don't want to have tea"

"It is not about tea Nuha, I can see somethings going within"

"What is your problem, I said I don't want to go, and you don't know me in and out that you would know what is going on within. I don't want to go for lunch or tea or talk to you or look at you. Please do me a favour and leave"

"Have I done something wrong? What has happened to you, what was this"

"No Veer, there is nothing wrong, just leave me alone"

I felt terrible when he left without a word, he never did anything wrong and I was so bad to him, a part of me died with this, I tried harder to let this thing go off my mind and focus on work but I could not. Just before signing off I messaged him,

"I am sorry, I did not mean to hurt you, I just wanted to explain that I cannot talk to you or stay in touch with you, please never reach to me on my mobile or here. Hope you understand."

I found the sticky note on my desktop the very next day, it said,

"I understand completely, but it is your turn to understand and act. Don't talk to me, I don't want that, just realise what you are into, this is not love. Stop blaming yourself for everything and settling for everything you don't want. Take care."

It was humiliating and embarrassing to even face Veer, deep inside I knew I was into something that was not love exactly but a bond that bounded, an agreement of sticking together for no matter what. But it was my choice, my choice out of love in the beginning that had slowly turned into choice out of my helplessness.

"Take one yellow capsule for your throat pain, and if you really feel anxious or stressed out take the white small tablet, and for nausea take the pink one. If you don't feel like sitting next to a male passenger, ask the hostesses to give you a seat near some lady, if that can be done" Adel was giving me all the necessary tips I would need during my journey, I heard everything in unison while my head was bursting with all the possibilities of things going wrong, all the kinds of accident that could take place. I hated traveling and of all I hated air travel. Air travel is scary, it has been that forever. I had explained Adel a millionth times but he did not listen to me, he thought my fears were illogical and he insisted me to go by air to my sister. Mumbai was one and half hour journey, but even that amount of time seemed like endless to me. I had visited my sister and dad previously but then Adel had accompanied me via bus journey, it was not easy but at least I could travel, since he was there by my side.

He would have accompanied me today but he had some family engagement which he apparently could not avoid. I bid him goodbye at the gate and checked in. He gave me courage that I can do it and I believed him. As soon as I boarded that boeing, I realised this was my biggest mistake, this time I shouldn't have believed Adel. Plane started moving on the runway, I had no company, both the side on either side was vacant and I freaked out. I wanted to scream and jump out of the plane but I was aware I would look so stupid if I acted badly. I consoled myself and the plane took off, I consoled myself with duas that I read, I made myself sure that nothing bad will happen, nothing bad will happen, I continued saying that to myself, I tried to look for people around, someone who could say me the same that nothing will happen and in that attempt my eyes rested on a child who was peacefully sitting on the lap of his mother. Look is he worried about anything, no, if there was something happening physically everyone would have been panicking, it is just in my mind, I need to take control of my mind and I kept talking to my mind, asking it to please understand as nothing would happen. I was sweating and freezing at the same time, one of the hostess crossed and offered me water. I accepted readily and drank it in one go, she asked if all okay, I said yes all fine, I didn't want anyone to know what my mind was fighting with. They would have laughed at me. I thought I should take medicine for anxiety but I did not, why I should rely on medicines, what if it did not work right and something goes worst. I did not even trust a medicine that was the level of my faith. My hand and legs were shivering, I wanted someone to hold me, I missed Adel, tears rolling over my cheeks and I held my face in my palm and bit my lips to keep myself together, I prayed God for I can't falter here, no one was there to hold me. I just wanted to live through this journey and never ever board it again. Just when a huge bump was felt and jitters all along the passenger area, this was it, it ended my patience and I lost my confidence over everything, I screamed and everyone was ogling at me, the hostess came running to me, she held my hand and asked not to worry, it was just a jitter and there is absolutely nothing to worry. She was holding my hand and that relaxed me, I was reassured that nothing would happen. I took a sip of water, I wanted to hide away from everyone, I couldn't believe myself to what I just did, I wanted to dig the plane and fly off, off from everyone's eyes and mind, I wondered what would they be thinking about me. Just then a mid age, tall man took a seat beside me, I was startled for a second

"Hi, I am Raghvendra, are you going to Mumbai too?"

Yes, I answered bluntly, where else would I go if not Mumbai, this plane terminates there.

"You know, I was claustrophobic myself, it was really difficult for me to travel by air or take a closed lift and it did hamper my growth and social life. I could not attend my best friend's wedding; I could not take travel projects from my company because I was afraid of travelling so much and for that matter, never dared to take any foreign trips."

And I listened to him very carefully, in my inquisitiveness I asked "so how did you overcome, how you are so comfortably travelling now."

He smiled at me as if he knew everything about me, he was talking exactly I wanted someone to talk about.

"I just surrendered to my fear, I decided to face it, I challenged myself as what could go worst, I would die, but death is inevitable, it shall come when it will and no one has control over that"

I nodded in acceptance.

"So once I started facing it, my fears were frightened and it ran away. See I am so comfortable today. So what do you do", he asked

"I work as a tax professional with a financial firm, and you"

"I work with the financial firm too but my profile is engineering"

"Oh! My sister is also an engineer, which college are you from"

"I passed out of IIT and then graduated from IIM"

"That is amazing, so you are one of the most sought out person of today's market"

"Yes I am, and pulled out his tablet to show me his daughter's pictures"

"She is so cute, what is her name"

"Avira, just one year old, I miss her so much while I am away for work"

"Yes, you would", and suddenly my ears started aching, I held my ears with both my hands, It is paining, I exclaimed.

"Oh that is because we are about to reach and as the altitude decreases, pressure increases, so due to that pressure we feel discomfort in our ears"

"You talk logic but my ears are hurting, I am afraid if something will happen, pain triggers my anxiety, and any kind of pain does."

"You know what my hobby is; I write songs and sometimes sing too", he ignored my complains

"You do, that is great"

"Would you like to listen to one?"

"No I am not feeling comfortable, I think I would puke."

"Relax and he plugged my ear with his headphones, and played his song"

It played–nothing's gonna change my love for you, you oughta know by now how much I love you..

That reminded me of the happy times we had as a family, when Sarah was around, when there was nothing I would fear, those times, how I wished I could turn the clock in reverse and wait for that time to return, that pain was more than any physical pain I would ever feel. I was lost in the words that played.

He poked me after sometime as I haven't yet introduced him my name, I opened my eyes and he was smiling, "we landed safely" and the pilot announced, "Welcome to Mumbai."

We bid goodbye to each other with a smile, he did not even know my name, he was a stranger but it seemed he knew me so well. He calmed me without knowing my history, without making me feel humiliated of my shortcomings. Such people are rare who give you so much in return of nothing at all. I wished everyone understood people's need without judging anyone.

Waiting outside to get the taxi, Adel called right when my mobile flashed signal.

"Are you okay? Reached safely, Oh I was so worried about you Nuha."

I wanted to scream at him that why did he force me to travel even when I tried so hard to avoid but I kept my cool and assured him of everything was good. How would I tell him, if that gentleman would have not helped me, I would have been in so much of trouble, I could have fainted, anything could have happened. I just thanked god for helping me through this and headed home.

Falak had left the keys beneath the doormat, I opened the door and the beautiful sight outside the wall sized window mesmerised all my senses. I fell like a star fish on bed and fresh air rejuvenated my soul. Her apartment was right at the foothills of Western Ghats, with a perfect view of lush Green Mountain and gulmohar tree in its full bloom like a blast of fire covered the place. I fell asleep instantly, only to wake up by continuous doorbell ring. I opened the door with one hand over my one eye, it was Falak. She gave a big hug and a cheerful squeak just like she has always been. I was too dull to respond to that and went back to bed.

In my deep slumber I felt like someone dragging me away from something I was trying hard to reach, oh! It was Falak, who held both my feet and was pulling me out from the bed, I cling to the corners of the bed and she tried harder, I gave up and got up.

"Why are you shrinking day by day, look at your friends, they look like your mom now" she grinned.

"Don't say like that, I am not well, you know everything, my life is nothing like my friends, and they are the lucky ones."

"Not well? What has happened to you? Doctors have taken all kinds of tests on you, they say you are perfect."

"I know that, but still I am not well, my brain is not good."

"You know that is not true, you are the most creative of all of us and that is only possible with a great brain."

"Creativity contributes to creative ways of developing fear and anxiety", I murmured and walked away ignoring her words.

She followed me, 'so what have you thought about, to be like this all your life, in a cocoon that Adel has built for you.

"Stop it, I have come here for some peace, it's my vacation, don't start it."

"Start what Nuha, you don't want to listen truth, what has happened to you, why have you believed that you are sick and depressed, it is like you are falling in the pit knowing how dangerous it can be."

"Look Falak, I do not have control over my mind, I know the rights and wrongs, I have logic but I am surviving and that looks like more than I deserve. You will not understand what I mean because no one is at my place. It is me, suffering not just because of my condition; I suffer watching people in misery around. I don't know what pills I took or where did I bang my head, I can't even look at a beggar at street, without tears in my eyes. Adel says I have become hyper sensitive to everything and I only know to shed tears. Tears can be seen, but my pain, no one sees that."

"I understand my baby sister; all I want is you as I know you not as what someone else expects you to be. You, like you were, one who could bring a smile on the saddest face. At least for the sake of Maaz and Mithi, they need us."

"I love them more than my life", I assured.

"No you don't, if you would have, you wouldn't be killing yourself in such a way. Think about Sarah, her kids are ours now, she has left to us, and we are the mother to those two. We need to give them so much that they never miss what is missing."

"I love Maaz and Mithi, they are like the reason to my life and hope of happiness."

"Then give them back, their mother, and real one who died for her children."

And everything played like a flashback in my mind, pain of loss pouring in my blood. It was never an accident, no cylinder blast, no mishappening. She was burnt in kerosene, alive, a cold blooded murder which was given an angle of an accident. Some said it was a suicide but no, Sarah was too strong to do that, she was a woman of substance, mother of two and a victim of bad marriage.

— x x x —

Chapter - 6

Revelation

I was back to Bengaluru, refreshed and with confidence.

There are people dying Adel, most importantly women dying because of violence against them, bad marriage, dowry, poor health, domestic torture, rape and pregnancy. How many families must be affected by that, are we supposed to just watch it and do nothing about it?

Why are you worried about it, I am not going to do anything like that, my parents might not like you that much as you are not up to their standards of religious belief but yes, they will never harm you.

I looked at him for a minute with tornadoes in my mind struggling to outpour, I said coldly–I was not just worried about myself, I was talking about people, real people who are being affected, just like me.

He noticed my strange cold attitude and held my face in his palm, " Nuha, no one can ever love you as much as I do, just remember that."

Why Adel, am I that worthless? I questioned back.

"No you are more important to me than you can be to anyone, I have accepted you in your worst, and no one can do this, I bet."

"Why didn't you try to correct me Adel, rather accepting me knowing it was bad for me, my health? Why this sacrifice from your side, I never wanted to be accepted, I wanted to be myself like I was."

"Why has your mind gone corrupted suddenly, is this some side effects of your recent vacation."

"No this is me", and I walked home alone that day.

That night he did not sleep, he kept on texting me how much he loves me.

"I love you my baby, I want to get married to you soon, it is just that I want my parents to like you that I ask you to be according to their demands."

"Goodnight Adel, I love you too J", I left a message for his security.

I felt the change in me; I would have never had the courage to say something against him and walking away alone was an accomplishment. Was it the reinforcement of Veer that assured me. I was still likeable and that Adel is wrong that no one can ever like me, or it was the courage I got from Sarah, her sacrifice making me uncomfortable in my comfort, her sacrifice screaming to take steps that I would have never otherwise. It was difficult to sleep that night but once I slept, it was peace. And peaceful sleep was rare gem in my life.

Early morning I got up to Adel's call

"Are you still sleeping, don't you have to go for work"

"I am just getting up, will go late"

"No get ready and come fast, I am waiting downstairs."

"Why are you here, I can take auto and I will take time to get ready, please leave"

"I am not leaving without you", and he hung up.

I had to get ready quickly and managed to take a sip of water, he was there, waiting under the sun to see me before he leaves for his work.

"Why did you have to do this", I shrugged my shoulder walking towards him

"I was missing you", he smiled

"Well, early morning"

"Yes, why can't I, were you not missing me"

How could I have said no and I nodded in positive.

"You look beautiful today, something special"

"No, I just felt good dressing up special"

"Yes, you must be missing all the attention I guess",

"I miss myself; let me do what I like to. And girls don't dress up to attract boys; it is a feeling, a sense of pride when we look good to our own eyes. When the mirror flashes the approved persona of you in your eyes, you then dress up with confidence and self love all over again. And that is important", I backfired.

He gave me that stern look of his and drove off without a word.

This scared me for a moment and I wondered what if he leaves me, he would certainly if I behave against his wishes. All along my mind thought about the worst, what love demands controlled action and enforced thoughts I wondered but again they say love is about sacrifice and compromise to stay together. I don't know how far is it the truth, but this is what I have been living from past two years. The only thing I was sure about was that I was not happy and yet I didn't have the courage to walk out of this.

He did not call me entire day, this was the first day in this entire period of relationship that he did not contact me for this long, it made me uneasy and this thought of not having him by my side suffocated me, dialed his number multiple times but he did not answer. I dropped a message apologising for everything that happened. I didn't understand what was I apologizing for, for being me or just a desperate attempt to make things fine, it did not convince me yet here I was begging for his forgiveness. He did not answer any of my texts or my calls. I had weird thoughts of being alone, what if I have panic attack tonight, or I fall sick and need him by my side, he wouldn't come for me. What if he leaves me in real, I will be alone, and who would marry me, who would accept me with all my issues. I wanted to divert my mind from all of these, I wanted to act normal, I wanted to be like the girl next door, who was so young, so charming, and carefree, most importantly self dependent. At that point of time, I wanted to be like anyone except me.

I took out my paint and drawing book that I had bought a year back to paint in my free times. Colours always fascinated me, how authoritative you feel when you have the power to create something, expose your imagination which you have been hiding out of fear of judgements. I painted one of my dreams, a man killing a woman, I carefully have drawn the expressions of their faces, the man was smiling wickedly and the woman was shocked and probably screaming in pain. There was a stream of blood flowing in the frame which I had darkened jungle red. And I slept without any anxiety episode in admiration of my creation that I controlled. It was fulfilling at the time when decisions of my basic functioning was not in my control.

I woke up to 16 missed calls from Adel, I called him back and he immediately picked

"Please don't go for work today, I need to meet you now"

I did not protest and agreed to that, "okay, will see you at 10 a.m."

He was there before time; we found a place in the nearby restaurant.

"Nuha, I am really sorry for the way I behaved with you, you know how much I love you, and how much I care for you, whatever I say or do is for your good. I want you to be happy."

"Do you really want me to be happy? Then please let me be myself Adel, I guess that way I will find my old self, a happy one."

"Just because I stop you from dressing up certain way and ask to avoid unnecessary contact with your friends doesn't mean I am not letting you be yourself. Where else do I lack?"

"You do not lack anything; you are perfect for someone but may be not for me."

"I have booked tickets for your favourite movie, please forget all these and let's go; we will have a good time."

"You know I don't go to theatres, why did you do so"

"You will be fine, trust me, now stop thinking and come with me."

I did not have an option further; we went for the movie, after all was my favourite animated movie. The dark space was packed with people, I could hear kids all around, and we found our corner seat and made us comfortable. He held my hand and asked if I was fine, I nodded and smiled, I do not know if he had noticed that in darkness. After half an hour he held me close and I rested my head on his shoulders, where I had taken refuge in my attempt to run away from everything that hurt, my most secured hide out.

He slipped his hand around my neck and I cuddled close, I looked at his eyes which were shining with the light of huge screen before us. I thought am I really in love or is it my incapability to stay alone that has kept me hooked till now. I was still thinking when he looked back into my eyes and bent to kiss my lips, he has never done that before, I was moved back immediately and he held my head tight and kissed me, he forced his lips over mine. I was breathless and moved him away with all my might. I looked at him for a minute and got up to walk out of the theatre. He came running behind. What's wrong, why are you behaving like this as if I am some stranger, I love you.

"You are no stranger but this is not what you ever wanted, what is wrong with you all of a sudden. You never wanted anything between us until marriage; it was your beliefs not mine. And this love of yours do not give you charge over everything of mine."

"Stop it, I am a man, I have needs and I want to make you mine in every way."

"All of a sudden what made you think this, until yesterday you wanted to avoid all kinds of sins and follow your principles. What made you change all of a sudden?"

"I can't lose you. I want you in every way. I want to make love to you, let you know how much I need you."

I had no answer to his changed behaviour. Of course we were in a relationship and everything he just said was reasonable, how long I would have escaped this. I was not ready for all this at this point of my life, who would have understood that and wasn't this my responsibility to cater to the basic needs of a relationship. We were not in an age old generation where couples could just make love through eyes million times before they actually got physical.

I had stopped feeling anything that would set butterflies in my stomach long back, anything that would excite me to the extent to fall in need to kiss or make love. My mind was never free from worries and fear of immediate troubles, how would I have thought about relationship in that angle.

That night he insisted to stay with him at his friend's place, I couldn't say no, how I deny him something he wanted, after everything he has been doing to me. And it was worthless to explain him the fact that I am not ready for all these, neither my mind nor my body had the will for love making or to have sex. I was tired because of being out all day, I just wanted to go to bed hold him tight and get a peaceful sleep. But there was something else in his mind, I don't know what had triggered in his mind, was he testing my love or my patience. He pulled me close and tried kissing, I turned my head other side and made it clear that I was not interested. He turned my shoulder to his side and moved his hand over my body, I hated to be touched like that; he did not care for my consent, I couldn't take such disrespect and I screamed at him.

"What kind of girl are you Nuha, are you a feeling-less shit head?."

"Yes I am, a shit head, a maniac, an abnormal girl, everything that you think of, I am a selfish person. I am sorry Adel, I am not sure if I love you or not. Or maybe I loved you initially but that probably faded in all these restrictions and rules laid by you on me. I do not hold any feelings for you of that sort, maybe I will never, you should probably find someone who is actually the person you want."

"Please leave me to my place; I want to go right now", I demanded

He calmed me, asked me to sleep that he will be dropping me home as soon as the day breaks and went to a different room.

I was left alone in that room to my disturbing thoughts.

I was helpless, I did not understand what was wrong with me, I wanted to scream at my helplessness and cry for my disability. I was unable to love the man I loved. He loved me selflessly, took care for me like a family would. He had made me his entire universe, made me his only priority and his reason to live. All his dreams, wishes started with me and ended to me. I felt miserable at how I had failed him, failed his love. I felt selfish and a crooked person who was just being with someone for one's own satisfaction, to seek support and be comfortable in my own created space. I didn't want anyone to disrupt that. Today when he demanded things he deserved, I failed, I was more important to myself than anyone in the world. I cared for myself and I was concerned about myself, I was worried about myself and I was just scared of everything that had potential to hurt me in any way possible.

One quality that I still held to from my past life was being impulsive and I did not know the following morning would change my life forever.

I walked out by 6 in the morning, came back to my place, got ready for office and reached before time. This company I worked for had brand image, people love to work for such prestigious name. It was the stepping stone of my corporate career, had I have taken it responsibly I would have only moved forward to excel in this field if my life was on a straight path. I wrote the resigning letter and before I could think much I had already hit send to my boss. I was not completely aware of the thing I was doing at that time, but I was sure, my conscience would not let me live with this image of mine, I could have lived being so selfish, I was just ruining Adel's life to worse by being in his life. I wanted to run away right away and never look back. He always wanted me to live according to his wishes, it was how he was, it was not his fault, it was my fault to choose that for myself knowing I wouldn't hold on to that, I do not possess that personality to fall into his criteria. It was me and only me responsible for my condition, my bad relationship, my bad physical and mental health. I didn't even try to get control over my life, emotions and decisions. I kept falling into everything that was served to me.

I waited for my boss to check his mail and find the resigning letter, of course it would come as shock to him, he had always liked me for the speed I work with, he wouldn't want to lose me and beside that, almost everyone was leaving from this team. Not because he was a bad boss as perceived by other people, he was the nicest man I had come across and a great boss. I would definitely miss him, with that thought of leaving the place made me sad, it was not that I was in love with the place, it was just that I was not ready for any change in my life and yet I was taking this drastic step, I had no clue about where would I go or what would I do. I felt like life was ending and there was nothing left in it. Of these, one thing I was very sure about was leaving Bengaluru and getting away from Adel.

I was once again running away from everything to find what I want, in this struggle of survival I wanted to be left alone for the very first time. I just wanted to run away.

"Nuha, I got your mail, can we go for a tea after sometime", my boss asked

"Yes boss, I will", flashing a dry smile at him.

I rushed to Sangeet, I was not sure if what I just did was right or another of my blunder. I narrated her whole story and waited for her response, probably something that would instill little confidence in me on my decision.

"Are you sure about this?"

"I don't know Sang, I just did it, yet to think about it."

"Ok, relax, this is the first time I have seen you doing something this impulsive, good or bad, we will just walk through, don't you worry"

She was a positive person and always knew what to say and what I did want to listen to.

"Okay times up, I will have to meet boss", and she wished me good luck

It was awkward going for tea alone as they always went for tea in a group. What reason would I give him, I thought all the way when I tried to figure out what actually do I want to do with my life ahead of this. And only one thing I could see, a new hope, maybe I will take up art and begin something from scratch, I have always wanted to be an artist.

"So, what is it Nuha, all of a sudden you decided to leave, is there any problem, feel free to share", boss asked

"No boss, I do just not like to stay in this city alone, also doctors are suggesting me to stay with family as I have repeated health issues."

"Okay, I understand, what would you be doing after this then?"

"I am figuring out, maybe I will join art school or something like that, I was always inclined towards all these so let's see, I will do something in that area, will be living with dad and my sister."

And our conversation continued for an hour, we discussed about everything, from things I like to my future plans, he opened up to me in a mysterious way and it was the most interesting talk with him. I loved every minute of that, although my heart was sinking as this would be the first and last of all.

Coming back, the news had already spread like fire, and Veer was the first one to ping me. I wanted to tell him personally but I couldn't get that chance.

"That was shocking, you leaving", Veer pinged

"Hmm, yes I have to. Thinking to join art school, I am tired of this city, probably need a change."

To my surprise he was positive about my decision without showing a slightest disagreement

"This is the best decision I will tell you, you were just ruining your life here, dulling your soulful charisma. I am happy you are doing something you want and not just someone else asked you to."

"Thank you" and I signed off.

That night I received Dr Adarsh's mail, it was something that instilled confidence in me for whatever happened during the day. It read

"Dear Nuha.

I know you are not going through a good phase; it would be great if you can take up some counseling sessions, you can also meet me on Wednesday/Saturday evening. I would also suggest you to give some time to yourself and spend time with family. You need not to worry, everything will be fine.

Regards

Dr Adarsh"

I slept determined and satisfied.

This too had an end, Adel might not have inflicted any wrong on purpose but he definitely had aggravated the pain I was in, nobody could have continued to live that way. I had to face him and let him know about all this. I was finally leaving the city and shifting to Mumbai with my sister. I met him.

"I am leaving Bengaluru, have resigned already"

"How could you do this to me", he was in a shock

"Do what Adel?"

"You are leaving me, you are leaving this place, and how can you just walk out of all these"

"Nothing is going good in my life here, I am not happy", I explained

"What about our relationship?"

"Adel, what is the point of this relationship when none of us are happy, I am not able to give you any kind of happiness, I am not the one you want. I couldn't change myself as you wanted me to.

This is what I really want, please don't stop me."

I could see he was in tears, he loved me, but his love was one in millions. You like a flower, so much that you want to hold it, keep it by your side, so you pluck it and keep it in the corner of your room, when it dries you keep it under the pages of an old book. You never want to lose it. I was just like that to him. He never wanted to lose me, all the hope and everything that was needed to keep me going was sucked out of my life, yet the most important thing for him was not my happiness but his, his satisfaction of having me beside.

Today when that was at stake he was bound to be violent. His outburst drifted me away and I was more than sure to leave everything to fight from myself. To explore the other side of me that I had forgotten existed in me. And to be honest I could not figure what was it between Adel and I, was it love, right or wrong. For the matter of fact when your entire world is falling apart, who cares about a broken heart?

— x x x —

Chapter - 7

Back to Mumbai

It was a drastic change in my life just like a fish taken out from the pond to an ocean, the vastness perplexes the fish. I was the same, I had immense opportunity to do anything that I wanted, but that was still a mystery to what I really wanted from myself. I needed time to figure out where my life was heading to. Falak, my sister's career was on the pinnacle, she lived a very busy life, travelling city to another, working late hours and I was doing nothing, staying home, cooking and watching outside the window which opened to a hill and a giant gulmohar tree. There was no one I knew around and there was absolutely no urge to even know anyone. I kept myself busy with my phone and laptop; those were the only outlet my life gifted to connect to the outside world.

Adel was not around, it felt insecure but relieved, I was not answerable to anyone, and there was no one to check on me, check my phone or guard on what I wear, where I go, what I do. I experienced freedom for real, freedom from all the restrictions, freedom from my own guilt conscience that I had built up on every little thing went against the protocol of his relationship. Though I felt bad for feeling fine but that was just momentarily, I was content and did not ever regret about leaving the city, Bengaluru.

I had all the time so gradually I came in contact with most of my friends on social media, they had isolated me because I had disconnected from everyone. It was a wonderful feeling getting back and knowing about their life. I remember I had spent nights on my friend's walls to read about their hitch up and checked out photos, there was a lot to catch up. Almost half of my contact list was either married or engaged; happy updates from everyone surrounded me and pushed me deeper in my negative thoughts about myself. It was a bitter realisation that when most of my friends are settling for life, I am here, doing nothing, ended up a relationship for good or bad and has absolutely no clue of what future holds for me. I was not a sadist, I was happy for them but I was equally unhappy for things in my life, after all they were my friends, I have grown with them, I deserved all those things that they had at this point of time. It made me feel sick and anxious about my own life; I started talking to people more often just to fit in, to feel important and included. I did not want to be left alone anymore.

Most of the times I was all by myself, I started painting, talking to my friends over phone, reading novels, decorating room, in my desperate attempt to keep myself busy I did everything I could. Still I was left with plenty of time and those were the times difficult to pass. Everything worst came to my mind in those time, what would my life become, where would I go after here, what should I be doing, I was even scared to step out of my house, how would I have ever be able to work and make my career. It was then when I missed Adel immensely, I missed his care and concern, how he was there for every little thing of mine, I just missed him without any desire to get back to him.

This was one such incident when I was all alone at home, I was watching outside my window and suddenly I heard a bang on my door, I was startled and thought about opening the door but then all the worst consequences came rushing to every nerve of my brain sending emergency signals. I gained courage and peeped through the eye piece, I could see no one there, I suppressed negativity and pacified my mind with reason, there are number of children playing around, someone might have banged and ran away for fun. I convinced myself and decided to do something, but it is really not easy to suppress a tornado that has already set out. I was holding paint brush to give a fine stroke on the half filled canvas and that was it, the colours on the canvas melted into one another and gave an illusion of the stormy ocean, it was blue then green and red, my hand started shivering badly, it turned ice cold in no minute. My heart beat was racing, fear gripped once again. Having no one around made this worst and I panicked, I rushed outside the apartment, I was on the stairs running away from the emptiness of that apartment. I called up Adel and he was quick to understand my situation, he called Falak and informed her while he was there all along over the call, he made me believe that nothing would happen and that I should not worry at all.

"Please Nuha, focus here, I am there for you, nothing can happen, just remember that"

"No Adel, you are not here, I am alone"

"But my dua is with you, God is there with you, I am not there physically but see I am there in every other way, you just don't disconnect the call."

"Rub your hands, and breathe in and out in a paper bag like the doctor had explained it to you, take a paper and curl it into a half circle and breathe in it."

"I am out, here on the stairs, I can't get up, I am scared Adel, something will happen to me. My heartbeat, look I am not feeling good."

"Get up Nuha, don't you listen to me, I am saying something, focus to that."

I got up, took a paper and took deep breathes, it was relaxing, Adel was there over the phone while Falak came. She came and I hugged her so tight as if I got my life back, she rubbed my hands and feet and made me lie comfortably while she sat beside me running her hand through my hair.

I was better, I felt everything was fixed back to its place, I felt like my life was granted back to me. And I held on it tightly, begging it to stay with me.

"Are you feeling better?, Falak asked

"Yes I am, I am sorry, you had to leave your work in the middle and come like this."

"It is okay as long as you are fine Nuha. Do you want to go out?"

I guess I would.

Falak was driving and I sat next to her in peace. It was just us but seemed as if my entire broken family is behind and it appeared I saw her in the rear view mirror sitting on the back seat. She looked pretty, there was no burn marks, her hair was loose in the wind and her smile was worth a million dollar. I did not want to turn back and ruin this beautiful, contended sight, I stared her and she stared back, we had so much to share but the language of eyes speaks huge epics in seconds. I loved Sarah.

I was brought back instantly by a jerk and Falak asked if I was okay. I was better and I smiled, I wished I could share what just passed my sight, but I didn't want to make her equally sad. This is the usual visuals I come across after every panic episodes, this is the thing that calms me down, helps me to settle with my restless inside. Sarah has been visiting in my dreams for years now, sometimes she looks so pretty and happy and other times she is perplexed, complaining. This was a secret I had saved from everyone; it was a personal space between me and my dead sister.

Falak has always been supportive, here she was leaving her work, helping me feel better and counseling me to get stronger.

"Nuha, you do not need anyone, you remember how brave you were once upon a time, and you are still the same girl."

"That was once upon a time Falak, but still I am fighting to get back to myself, told me."

"You don't have to fight, you have to settle everything even, I beg you just come out of this, everyone needs you, think about Mithi and Maaz, they need you. Think about Sarah, would she ever want you to become like this."

"She wouldn't, but she shouldn't have left us. That is what went wrong. She should have stayed."

After a long silence I noticed Falak wiping her tears off, she was equally disturbed but she has learned, learned to use her strengths in adversity. She was responsible and the strongest girl in this young age, she was trying hard to stitch back the broken family into one. I knew the pain she was in, but I was helpless, my uncontrolled, unwanted anxiety issues had reduced me to a worthless human being.

In this whole interlude, I knew I had committed a blunder. I had called Adel, asking for help. It was selfish of me but then it was only him who could have understood my situation, he has been there, suffered along by my side. This guilt of disturbing his existence was eating me up too and I texted him apologising for the call.

To my surprise it appeared that he was eagerly waiting for this situation, he did understand the reason why I called but he overlooked everything and started accusing me of using him for my own selfish reasons and that I never loved him. I couldn't have denied his allegations, I had called him for that same support, I didn't call him when I was missing his presence, when I was missing his concern, and I was selfish. I wanted to run away from him and at the same time I was the one needing him. He was not kind with his words he used for me and that hurt, it hurt but somewhere I believed I deserved that, making it comfortable with those vengeance. It is us, human mentality to distort what we cannot possess, to ruin the existence of something if that do not benefit us. I was the victim of his hatred; he ruined the respect he had in my eyes with his constant hate inflicted on me in different ways. I was the betrayal, for him and he made sure I pay for that.

I confessed Adel same thing again and again that I do not love him and I definitely don't want him because I was not the one he wanted and he continued to abuse and blame, while I continued accepting everything that came. After all everything he said was somewhere true and if not true, it well fitted to the condition. He didn't care about my situation anymore, he didn't understand that I was not selfish as a person, but my anxiety had made me selfish, extremely concerned about just me because my survival was at stake, every day I lived with fear of ending forever. He did not know that or may be did not consider that it to be any serious.

Months passed by and I kept struggling each day, escaping Adel's curse and my disability. I spent time with books and took up blogging; I wrote everything that hurt, I wrote about my incapability, about relationship, about hate and about respect. I wrote about women, her desires and her freedom from patriarchy. Every single word of hatred from Adel turned out to be a lesson learned. He was in an illusion that he was making me realise my mistakes but the reality was different, I was learning, my fragile soul was polished with tar and concretes, I was under construction.

Gradually I was pushed away and gained confidence in my decisions of having walked away from him. Because the sky was clearer after monsoon, someone who really loves you will not pitch into destroy you, will never stop respecting you. I believed his love was his obsession and nothing more than that.

My life was monotonous, but I had now come to terms with it. I had learned to tackle mild disturbances of my brain all by myself. I didn't need anyone's help for that, I was able to stay busy with my work all alone and there were few nights when Falak had to travel outside the city, I managed myself. It made me feel good and this encouraged me to believe on myself more. Maybe I was deceiving depression and crawling out of it or maybe not.

— x x x —

Chapter - 8

Ryan in My Life

Amidst all this, I didn't even realise who crept in my life silently; he was an old friend from my high school. We had come in contact through common school group and lately it was him, I slept talking to. I talked to him for two reasons, he had a picture of me that I was desperately searching for, my old self and second, he made me feel important and wanted at the time I was considering myself worthless in my eyes. He used to narrate history where I was the centre of his narration and I loved being drunk in that, I slept peacefully in its high and woke up fresh in its hangover in those days.

Can I ask you something, Ryan texted me early morning.

He was a girl charmer, native of Himalayas, white like Himalayan snow and tall like chinars. His broad shoulder gave him the edge of a hunk looking man. I remember back in school days, he had proposed me in the most awkward way, his hands were shivering before me and his white face had turned red with blood rushing in unison. It was something beautiful I had ever experienced, now he laughed talking about all that while I felt like living those back again, once again.

His question struck the same cord and shook me from inside.

"Can we give us another chance, I have been in many relationships in past but it was never how I had first felt with you, I could never stopped loving you, you went away from me but I always kept your track because you were really never out of my mind."

I read the message twice and thrice, I read it number of times to assure myself, it is really what I was reading. I was in awe, I liked everything lately, I liked talking to him, and I liked how he treated me as if I am some precious gem of his long lost treasure. Why wouldn't I have liked it, when it gave me so much of peace and smiles, this is what I was lacking in my life, my smile and I found that here in him. Just when my mind was pulled by his goodness, reality lashed on my face and I questioned myself, "what about Adel?"

And I saw myself divided into, a pessimist and an optimist one.

"What about Adel, why are you even thinking about it when all he thought was how could he exploit your weaknesses to make you exactly the way he wanted", the inner me screamed in me.

"Yes, you were a puppet he adored"

"But, what about his concern for me, his sacrifices and everything he did for me, the other me opposed."

"Were you happy being with him."

"No I wasn't, but what if he comes to know about it, I cannot do anything without letting him know. I just want he should know everything that I do."

"Will he be happy knowing this or was all the curses not enough for you that you want to give him more reasons to abuse you."

This was the hardest moment of my life and I was torn between opinions of my mind. Here again, my pessimism won and I decided to decline his proposal. Things that were long back in my life hold no place in my entirely changed life at present.

"Nuha, are you there, whatever it is you can tell me", he messaged once again and I started typing immediately, I was determined, Adel was not the only reason for my determination, my shortcoming was the major reason to deny this happiness to myself because I knew I would not be able to hold it for long, he would find my flaws and drift away. I wanted to stay as same in his picture, same desirable girl, I couldn't have destroyed that, picture of my good self.

"I like us together, I have always. But I do not want to start what I cannot end, it isn't possible between us, hope you understand", I texted him with a heavy heart.

"No I did not understand, I know you liked me and even now you are so happy with the way things are between us, what is the problem then."

"There are only problems Ryan, you don't know the truth and you will want to run away from me the moment you get to know."

"Whatever it is I want to know right now and nothing can set me apart from you this time, God has given me this one last chance to fix my life, please don't ruin this."

"You are better off without me because I don't want to wreck your life in future, I know everything looks good initially but then relationships break, happiness fades and all that is left is painful experiences."

"Look Nuha, I do not want to know about your past, don't even want to know about those painful experiences, I want you to be yourself as you are now and I assure you all the happiness of the world."

"It just sounds so easy when you say that but my past is not the only thing, I have my own issues, I don't think I am fit enough to be in any relationship, please understand."

"Why do you think so, whatever it is, can't we just work upon that? I know I am really being obsessive but I want you to know I desperately want you."

I decided to tell him, "I am suffering from depression; it's been two years now. Please don't take this lightly because there are instances when I do not understand myself, I get extremely aggressive and at times compulsive sadness overtakes. I do not smile often, I fear almost everything, I get panic attacks which becomes really difficult for anyone to handle it. I doubt on everything, even when you said about your feelings, I liked it but I did doubt your intention. Sometimes I am motivated to cure myself and at times I give up all hopes and struggle to sleep. I do not know about the sun next day, that hopeless I become. I am never happy, what happiness would I give you."

I messaged everything that came in my mind at that point of time; I felt the need that he should know about my flaws or my incapability. I didn't want him to reply to this and to my surprise he didn't answer. Although my mind asked me to stop expecting any replies my heart yearned for a simple hello, as all these days it was him in every hour of my day.

My phone ringed at the middle of the night, I watched it ring and missed at first, it rang twice and my hand immediately swiped it right.

"Hello?"

"Why are you still up" he asked

I had no answer to his why, I pretended as I was just about to fall asleep and he called.

"Please listen to me carefully, everything that I say", his husky voice mesmerised me, and his authoritative tone did not disturb me. I wanted to listen to him unlike my usual self. I had given up listening to anyone because I had it enough already.

"when I first saw you in our school days, the moment you had walked in with that confident aura, I had fallen for you right there, after that I never came across a girl for whom I felt the same. It was not my time, then, but I know it is now, you might be sick, your head might not be fine but here I love you for the person you were, you are and you always will, Nuha will remain the same at every phase of her life and I will love her same."

"Are you listening to me", he reassured.

"Yes I am", I whispered, I followed his every word and wandered in time he took me to. I was falling in love with myself again.

I was hardly out of a relationship, partly because of the person I was with and partly because I was too depressed to stay in love. But then, why Ryan did attract me so much, for that very moment I was not worried for anything else. Though my mind was meddled with thoughts of fearful fate and disastrous end, I was sailing like a wrecked ship unfretted and fearless.

— x x x —

Chapter - 9

Ryan Visit Mumbai

We spent months talking over phone, talking about Mumbai rain to Delhi heat, talking about things that made no sense. Talking about how beautiful I look in pictures, which were probably enhanced with beauty apps, about my job, his job, my friends, his friends and our friends. We talked about their marriage, kids, love stories of people who were once around us. He talked about his past relationships and I never had the courage to do so.

I felt as if I had given up the struggle on surviving and have started living, my days were happier and nights were romantic, I thought this is it, my happiness I was longing for. He is the change my life needed; I had no panic attacks for months in the history of last two years. Falak noticed and without any serious intrusion she was just happy knowing my positive changes. This was new and unexplored realm of my universe and I was enjoying every bit of that.

One day, an unexpected message belled my phone.

"I wish I could see you for real, slip my hands around your waist and kiss you on your lips. It's the only thing I wish for lately, all the time"

I was bewildered on his text and wanted to call and check if it was really him, we never had such kind of conversation in four months of relationship and all of a sudden, also my first doubt was what if it is not him and someone else would have texted me.

I called up immediately and he answered in his signature tone – Yes baby

"Did you just message me, I thought may be someone else was the other side."

"You are talking to me shona, who else would be there, and why do you think I can't message you like that."

Yes he loves me, then why can't he, my mind questioned back to myself. It was fair enough to expect such things when you are into a relationship, even if you are not ready for the same, even if your conscience doesn't allow, your consent has no say because he loves you. It reminded me of Adel somehow.

I questioned him on why did he message like that, it was little uncomfortable all of a sudden. He replied in his grumpiest mood that I have ever seen, you totally spoiled my mood, I am really sorry, I will never ever do that again.

And I couldn't feel more guilty for having him feel that way, dejected, so I apologized and lighten up the scene accepting that I wanted to kiss him as badly as he wanted me to.

"I want to see you and that is all, I want to meet you in person and know that this feeling this relationship is for real", he messaged and one could make out that he had that urgency to meet and it was quiet natural. I wanted to meet him the same, the only difference was that I was too lost in present to take things forward; you can say I was crippled to think beyond now.

And finally we decided on meeting, discussed and fantasised everything about our first date. I was super excited for everything that was scheduled and kept in store for me. He planned the Mumbai visit with friends from school; we thought it to be a school reunion too as it's been years we last met. Tickets were booked and we waited for each other like madness, from there on all we discussed about was our meeting, how magical it will be, things we would do and places we will visit together. Thought about visiting places sent chills but I did not want to make that evident and ruin things for him, everything was so beautiful that it lacked space for my ugliness, my depression.

Finally the day arrived, he asked me to visit a mall in Goregaon, a few kilometres away from my home in the evening. While my mind rambled, after years I would get dolled up today, put on my favourite dress and shiny stilettos, maybe I will wear little make-up, just a bit to cover my dark circles I have earned in these years, would add little glow to my cheeks that have faded it's natural pink. Yes I will manage and I came out of shower with a new confidence.

Even though every time I saw myself through his eyes, I fell in love with myself. I wanted to get ready and watch myself look at my best; I put on my sexy lacy bra that would go with my black dress. I don't even remember when I last wore these kinds of my favourite outfits. It was a long dress, not so sparkling, and moved like fluid, it was exactly like a princess would wear on her evening date. I wore makeup and red lipstick, I looked dreamy in my mirror, I was actually living the kind of ideas I always had in my mind and those I wrote in my journal. I put on my shoe to rush out, just then I remembered I had to leave home and travel those 10kms all by myself in a taxi. How perfect everything was just before this thought, my mouth dried and struggled to gulp my saliva, I knew it was overpowering me. I drank water, lots of water, sat down and took three deep breathes in a paper bag. I don't remember how long I kept sitting there just in that position hoping it to go away. I begged to myself, not today, it was supposed to be my good day, but all in vain, I kept feeling nervous, my palms felt the blood rushing and feet turned cold. I read my duas that Adel had taught me to read when I panicked and no one is beside. I wanted to call Adel and tell him about this, I was restless and needed help. But this was not the day to give up, I assured myself I will be fine, tears rolled down and my kohl smudged, tears ruined the blush of my cheeks and water washed away my lip colour. I was about to give up when Ryan called.

Where are you, we have reached here, how long will you take?

I couldn't have ruined this, he had come all the way from Delhi, and we have lived this moment in our conversation for millionth times, I did not want to take this away from him. I gathered courage and stood up on collapsing heels, "I am coming, was just leaving".

"Okay we are waiting" and he hung up.

I had to go, I had no other option, I fixed my face and held my heart, locked my apartment, checked it twice and walked towards the lift, I had no problem with the kind of lift it is in Mumbai's buildings, it is open from a side and you can see through that. A small kid who was sharing the lift stared at me with a smile, while we were stepping out of the lift, she broadened her smile and said–"you are looking so beautiful di."

I smiled back at her and headed to take the taxi. It was dark by now, birds were chirping on a very high note, aunties of the society were sitting on the pavements and gossiping and while I walked past they stopped their gossips and looked at me from head to toe. It could be for any reason, may be because they had never seen me like this before or maybe they actually found me beautiful. For whatever reason, I was feeling beautiful and that really made me confident.

I stopped a taxi and confidently took the back seat hiding the terror inside with a fake stubbornness on my face. I immediately made a call to Ryan and informed that I was on my way and mentioned that I have taken the taxi safely. He was not really concerned about that it seemed yet I gave him all the details as I was used to do so.

I called and informed Falak about it and also specifically told about the place I had hired taxi from, I wanted to give her the details of that taxi too but I could not check it prior. I have read news of abduction and cases of sexual assault of women, I wanted to make sure I was safe; my anxiety had made me obnoxious and restless on every little thing. Any small thing that might not even gain attention of a normal person would be one of the major causes of my worry. In a way this had also helped me in taking extra care of myself and being alert all the time, but this has the worst side too as you really not live in the present, you live in the world of uncertainties, digging to find the wrong in anything perfect, in the world of what may go wrong.

The weather was perfect when it started raining and the road was jam packed, no vehicle moved, and I became restless again. I called Ryan and described the situation bit by bit, I just wanted him to be there on the other side so that I do not freak out and embarrass myself. He may not have understood and after listening to everything he disconnected the call saying "reach soon, I am waiting".

I scanned my phone to keep myself hooked to something, I fidgeted, lowered the window glass, and my behaviour was loud if not clear of what was going on in my mind. The driver must have been observing me since long and must have read my discomfort.

He turned and my heart skipped a beat,

"are you okay madam, this rain causes traffic jam, just a few more minutes and you will reach"

"I know", I answered rudely, I didn't want to give him any friendly gesture, any signal that could be misinterpreted to harm me. But people do hurt when they hurt, all they look for is an opportunity, like the time when I was just an eight years old girl, I was a kid, he had grabbed me from behind and scratched my flat chest making sounds I did not understand. I did not give any signal when he had turned my head to bite my lips so hard and my mouth smelled beetle leaves, since then I had hated that smell, I hated that teacher. I could never talk about it to anyone, I didn't know what words would I have used to explain it to someone. I had that picture of men in my mind and the same thought was for the taxi driver too.

He did not turn back to talk to me further and I lowered the window glass for both the sides, I wanted to keep a way out in case he misbehaved, the journey of a few minutes turned into hours. I was agitated for I was not able to reach to him and this traffic was really testing my patience. I called him and he complained and I explained, it was not my fault, I had no idea about the traffic at this time, I just wanted to see him right there.

As my destination neared my nervousness turned into excitement, this kind of anxious mind did not hurt me, it just made me happy because I was going to see him after six years and that too first time after coming into this relationship. I was worried how would I react and my behaviour, how would I face him, would I shake hand or smile or just say hello. It was all mixed up, I paid the bill and thanked God for I reached safely, I tried to fix my messed up hair and headed towards the entry taking quick small steps.

I stood there and looked around for him, I had not forgotten his face but it was difficult to spot him in that crowd and I hoped he would find me like he has really found me. I turned around to a tap on my shoulder, it was Yash, I flashed a smile and he smiled back.

"Why are you so late", he enquired

"Oh! Don't ask, traffic and rain, it ruined everything. I was still looking around while answering to him."

"Who are you looking for? He left; he was really tired because of the journey."

"Ryan left?" I asked in the saddest tone to which he burst into laughter.

Ryan joined him in their "funny moment". I watched him in a way someone would look at their dream coming true. He was too shy to look at me directly and it was too tempting for me to not look at him. I wanted to hold this moment to myself as it took me to the corridors of memories, the classroom romance, and meeting of eyes followed by skipping of hearts. It was absolutely the same, the innocent summer love.

That moment I could not hold myself, it was like as if I wanted to run away and never see him again or maybe run into his arms and never leave it. When the mind and the body is in such unison, we really don't know how to react and end up in some loud unacceptable behaviour. So was with me, my subconscious mind acted weirdly, over confident and loud. I made lots of hands movement while explaining the delay, traffic and rain, I wanted to act normal while my inside was crushing to pieces, my heart racing faster than the time, lips were dry and I had to hunt for words to speak out loud. Ryan must have read line behind my words and he spoke in the kindest voice – "shall we eat something, I am really hungry." So we walked to a restaurant nearby and booked the table for three. He sat by my side and shuffled the menu while I tried to make things comfortable around; I started a conversation with Yash about his life and career. Sitting just beside him had made me super conscious of everything. I was doing, talking or feeling. I never knew my heart held such melodramatic me within. But I could see his discomfort too, trying to catch a glimpse but not being so obvious. When I caught him twice or thrice watching, staring at me, may be hunting for the differences and similarities when he had seen me last, 6 years back. It did rip me off; I was not ready to be seen or evaluated, it turned me red and my eyes blurry. Stop shooting me with your eyes, I am submerged in embarrassment and drunk in the magic of love and romance, my heart screamed.

After the wonderful dinner, where I ate everything out of my nervousness and they did not eat anything out of awkwardness we walked out and it was still raining heavily. I really had to move out of this place because the place, the crowd, the noise, too many things at a time was freakishly uncomfortable and was just adding to my anxiousness. I almost forgot about my anxiety stricken mind just before leaving the house a few hours ago. Here I was too busy to bask in the bliss of my first encounter.

Somehow we managed to hire a taxi and Ryan decided the destination to a sea beach, although it was my city, I was supposed to be the host but everything was as new to me as to them. But I was well aware of Mumbai monsoon, I warned that it was not a great idea, beach in the monsoon night, but Ryan was determined so I gave up as all I wanted at that very moment was to run out of that place to some quiet distant one where I can hide my emotions and conceal passion.

How on earth would I have known it will surge out like a hurling machine before him, the moment I would sit beside him at the back seat of taxi? Yash took the front seat and took in charge of the music while starting a friendly chat with the driver. We were left alone to ourselves for the first time that day; it was the torment I was dreading all these days, what would I speak to him when it is just us, how would I react to things he would ask me, compliment me, all those things that we have talked about over the phone in past 6 months, it was all running mad in my head. I looked away outside the glass window, the fast moving buses, street lights passing like a streak of light, and his blushing face in my mind. I wanted to strike a conversation about anything, just to kill this silence between us, I wanted to let him know how glad I was that he visited but my courage gave up and I waited hopelessly for him to talk to me, and he did.

All of a sudden without speaking a word he held my hand, I turned to him in a fraction of second as if someone had swiped me off my feet or blown me on the hot air balloon. I was nervous, I was scared, not for he was holding my hand but I knew from here on, I will no longer be the same person who has locked her feelings and drowned it in the beds of the weedy pond. I knew I will not be able to hold on to myself anymore, my eyes questioned him why did he touch me just like the time he had confessed his feeling in our English class, he once again made the same place in the deepest part of my heart.

My heart was pounding, splashing my feelings on to him. I was breathing heavily, my gasping for more air and my chest like the rivulet up and down. Oh! Please stop, I begged myself until my eyes fixed on him for the first time that night and my hand slipped harder into his hand. I locked my eyes onto his and asked million questions without saying a word. Trust me whoever said this, it cannot be any truer, eyes do communicate. I wanted to ask what took him so long to find me back, for keeping me distant from the feeling I deserved, this intense feeling.

I wanted to ask him right then and there about everything, about how I looked like, will he love me forever for who I am and not want something from me that I am not, if he will be my prince charming that I used to read about in fairy tales, will he stop here with me, will he be the same everyday from now on, will he be my partner in all sickness and health, happiness and sorrow, will he allow me to dream that was crippled by someone in past. This was me, weaving another story worth to be rewritten. I was still fixed to his eyes when he pulled me closer to his face, so close that I couldn't see anything and my eyes were shut and he kept me holding by my waist for a long time, had I have moved a centimeter ahead, I would have ended up kissing his lips, his vicinity made my breathe heavy and the harder I controlled, miserably I failed. Probably he sensed it and released his forceful hand but it was like as if I was glued to him I couldn't move back. And my head fell on his broad shoulders, I wanted to dig in there and hide somewhere inside, I held his shirt tightly and tried to calm my heartbeats. It was the most satisfying feeling, when my brain was tranquilised and my smile was constant, smiled in the belief that I had found the one, the first unconscious choice of my heart. If today, tomorrow or years after someone will ask me to define love, I will narrate this. This feeling without a space of belief, logic, right or wrong, obligation or tradition, this will remain my perfect definition of love.

We reached the iconic Juhu beach to find the sea swelled up, it was ready to swallow anything and everything on its way. We found a dry space to sit for some time, I had to return early as this was the first time I was outside my house at this time of the night. I constantly nagged about leaving early and he seemed to be having the best of his moments, he was sitting right in front of me looking at me like a dream without speaking a word and I was struggling to escape his eyes. I looked above and after like ages found stars in the monsoon sky, like a child I pointed the arrow constellation I always have observed since a long time. I got a few minutes of distraction to fix my messed up hair by cool mesmerising wind of the seaside. I was enjoying, finding goodness in everything around so unlike me, my brain kept all negative thoughts at bay effortlessly. This was his magic I was living.

We strolled by the sea side and he held my hand, I could not look at him at this point as I was too shy and he was way taller to reach.

"Nuha, I wanted to tell you something, I came here to see you, just you."

I smiled and said "I know that, why else would you have come."

"Also to tell you something I could not have said over the phone with 1400kms distance between us."

This sentence made me nervous and the first thing that came in my mind was negative for sure, maybe he wants to break this relationship and has come to console me.

"Please take everything very seriously, whatever I say."

I nodded

"I have come to get hold of you, to make myself believe that you are really there, for real. I have lost you once; I cannot afford it second time because it will be the end of my life."

"What are you saying, why would you lose me, I am here."

"Marry me", he interrupted.

And you do not know how dramatic the monsoon is, it was actually drizzling and I was not running to escape drizzle that had covered my face and my head. I was in awe, it was surreal and the same time so real, I went into his arms without making any conscious decision to do so. He held me close and I closed my eyes pressing my face deep in his arms. I did not want anything more after that, it was my perfect moment. All I could say was,

"I have risked my eternity and beyond, guard it as it is all yours."

It was 12 a.m., ideally I should be home by now but here I was in his arms. If only I could hold this moment forever but no I was never really able to. We talked for another few minutes and he called a taxi to drop me home. My leather jacket was wet and was irritating my body; I removed it and made myself comfortable sitting next to him. I was trying untangling my messed up hair but it was so bad that I gave up, I looked at him and he made me blush, he was not ready to take his eyes off me. I pushed his face other side and he got it back on me. In my embarrassment I asked what is it and in the most romantic voice he complimented for the first time

"You are the most beautiful woman"

Oh stop it! I blushed again and he held my cheeks. I was terrified being this close to him; my heartbeat raced the Olympics once again. He came closer and I closed my eyes, he rested his lips on my lips and I did not move, I did not know about a thing around, it was all dark and psychedelic. I did not move my lips and he pushed his lips onto mine. Neither of us was ready to pull oneself back and we ended up in a minute of lip kiss.

'You shall remain the first unconscious choice of my heart', my voice shuddered for I was soaked in the thunder of our first kiss. I pushed him away while I looked outside the window, a slight smile crossed my face and I could still see the ocean outside. My passion was vast like this ocean and wild like the high tide waves.

It was the hardest goodbye, he wished me goodnight and I walked towards my building. He waited there until I reached my apartment and informed him. Falak was fast asleep, probably tired of the journey that day. I wanted to wake her up and narrate everything that happened, everything I felt and the most special thing that he proposed for marriage. I lied down on my bed in charm of the time I just had, I wanted to think about my life with him ahead, and I just wanted to be happy for everything. But my mind was so in peace that I fell asleep.

It was the last day of his trip, my heart was sinking for it would be months before I could see him again but I was equally glad as I got to see him. That day I had invited all of them on lunch without having any clue about cooking but I managed to prepare some ready to eat food. I was in total mess when there was a knock at the door, I looked at myself and I looked devastated but it didn't matter to me, I rushed to open the door. There he was looking handsome as usual, his charming smile compensated for all the trouble I had taken to prepare a substantial meal for them. He looked at me and I looked deeper in his eyes, lost in the magic moment.

Let us at least come inside, you both can have this stare game later, Yash grinned and it made me blush.

All of them settled with things that could keep them busy and started their conversation without any direction while I rushed to kitchen and then back forth just like a perfect host. Ryan noticed how perplexed I was about everything so he accompanied me to the kitchen to help; this was the first time we were to ourselves. I turned to add sugar to the kheer and he held me from behind, I dropped the can on the floor and tin can ringed on the floor loud. I was startled and so was he, he asked if I was okay and I bit my lips for acting so weird and stupid. He held my hand and calmed me and promised he won't touch me. I was relaxed, although I could not handle that situation very tactically, it was actually one of those incidents out of my dream book where I had fantasised him there a number of times in the pink of my feelings.

He helped me arrange the dishes and serve everyone. Yash never miss commenting on such occasions and here he was once again, "looks like you both are a married couple and we have been visiting for lunch". I smiled because that was actually I felt like and I wish it was true right at that moment without going through any melodramas of possibilities and impossibilities. I wanted to watch him eat, watch him sleep, watch him watch me and a lot more, every time he looked at me with his side eye he caught me watching him and that made me comfortable but I was so madly in love with him I couldn't help myself.

And then something happened which I dreaded the most, Yash and others decided to leave for some work nearby while Ryan asked if he can stay back for the time they return. I did not know what should I answer, I wanted to deny out of fear and I wanted him to stay out of alien feeling of my gut. In my indecisiveness he stayed, that was the most uncomfortable moment when I was left all alone with him.

I could see his deep black eyes shining like a black pearl wandering and then fixed on mine. If looks really kills then those were the ones. I knew somewhere in the middle of those looks and the silence that has crawled, the torment of passion was right there to attack.

He walked towards me, words drew closer and in no time I could hear his whisper, "I love you mad", I looked into his eyes while his hands wrapped around my waist pushing and pressing against his torso, his broad tough shoulders rested my tiny little head. It was when I felt complete, something fulfilling, when nothing else crossed my mind, when thoughts just disappeared and it was me and him sailing the beauty of emotions gushing through every cells of our bodies.

Yes this was it, the moment I can cherish my entire life, the ones which will go to the pages of my diary. And those were all real, not a sort of meager imagination. He lifted me in his arms like a cotton ball and kissed me intensely, so intense that I don't remember when did we reach the bed. I was lying on my bed, heavy breathing, heart beat rushing, and all I could see was his vigorous look shooting over me. We looked into each other's eyes and it was the most romantic thing, he relaxed me and we lied facing each other.

He was lying beside me running his fingers through my hair and we did not talk for quite a while, and stayed in our thoughts. However I broke the silence and asked him

"Don't leave me Ryan."

And he turned to me, kissing my forehead answered in his hoarse voice, "I love you and how can I leave you when I have found you after such difficulties. I smiled at him and hugged him tight, I was convinced in forever once again.

— x x x —

Chapter - 10

Chamak

Ryan left to Delhi and I was left here back to my schedule, texting and calling to keep up the spark, having met him for real, I was more confident and happy now. My anxiety attacks dropped and I started looking up to beautiful things, things that never appealed in past was poetry now. The idea of being together in a life term relationship slowly sync down my system. My flaws and shortcomings were no longer disturbing to my mind; I was turning to positivity and accepting life. Falak was also happy about the changes and she wanted me to heal completely, with this idea she suggested me why don't you go out and explore the city. I was skeptical about it at first but then on her constant push I decided to go out on one Friday. It was the month of October, monsoon was withdrawing and one could feel the fresh breeze and I could feel the new beginning for so many reasons. I was happy.

I wanted to try local train of the city therefore took an auto to Kandivali station, I thought I will take the western line and travel to church gate, I always wanted to visit the massive state library that was in the Colaba region and planned to give my dad a surprise visit at his workplace in Worli while returning. So many plans in my mind, I informed Ryan and he was happy as I was taking initiative to bring required changes in me. He asked to keep him updated and call if I face any problem, it was obvious he could have not done anything sitting 1400 km away from me at times of need but those words were an encouraging enforcement and much needed confidence to action the plan.

There was a long line at the ticket counter, so I got in the queue and waited for my turn, the line moved really very slow and that took toll on my patience, I checked my phone repeatedly, refreshing my facebook page to check for notification. I wanted to call Ryan but did not as he was at work. I distracted my mind until I reached the counter, the man asked single return or one way, I asked for return without knowing what it meant. After receiving the ticket I realised it is for both the ways, which was a relief thinking I would not be waiting for tickets anymore for that day.

I checked for the platform and headed towards it, I was told that since it was afternoon, there would be less rush but that was not the fact, it was still crowded. I somehow managed to board the ladies compartment, it was comparatively less crowded than other compartments, luckily found a corner to sit as my legs were already tired of all waiting in the queue for tickets. Two stations crossed, third crossed and by the time I reached Goregaon, I felt cold feet to go further, I wanted to get down, take a taxi and return home but doing that would mean I lost once again. I stayed very firm at my decision to reach Churchgate and tried to read people around, get indulge in small vendors at the compartment, people were checking out hairpins and artificial jewellery. I tried to act normal and looked at the anklets hanging on their display, it was full of stars and I can never deny stars, they are my favourite, I asked for the price quote and the small boy quoted it for ₹ 20. I was amazed as the design and the material was too good to be that cheap so I readily paid him and pocketed my anklet. It was metal shiny and it was stars. This was a good food for my mind as I reached almost half of the journey; I was relaxed than before and waited for the last station eagerly, thought of this accomplishment kept me going.

I got down at Churchgate station and walked outside the gate but that was it, the moment I stepped out I had a head rush, felt like I haven't got down of the train, the movement in my head still kept rushing and I sat down there itself. I was aware of the few eyes rolling over me, but I could not help, thought of having no one familiar around made it worst and I lost it completely. I pulled my phone and wondered whom should I call, many thoughts crossed my mind, if I call my dad he would not be able to take the stress and Falak was too far away to reach me. I rubbed my hands together and tried breathing deep when a hand reached my shoulder and I turned in utmost fear. She asked me "are you okay?"

This question itself was of relief even if it was from a complete stranger.

"No, I am scared. I replied at once without analysing the person, without thinking anything else."

She held my hand and made me sit on the bench nearby, she offered water, I denied and took out my own bottle to drink water, I took a sip and thanked her for the help.

"Where do you want to go?"

"I came to visit State Library here in Colaba."

"Oh! That is a beautiful structure, you will love it."

"Have you been there? I asked out of my curiosity."

"I have seen but never been inside. But I am sure it would be massive and amazing."

Why didn't you go inside, do you like reading? I asked in my innocence. She was well dressed, with heavy makeup on her face; she was a pretty looking woman wearing burgundy lipstick which was the centre of attraction on her foundation layered skin. There were scars on her neck which she tried to cover with her scarf. Her deep necked top revealed her cleavage and she pulled it very comfortably. And without any further judgement I had assumed she was a literate until she answered.

No, I never went to school but I always wanted to get in that library and know what is inside, suddenly she hung her head and said, I do not even hold any identity card, they demand for one at the entry.

I wanted to ask what does she do, but did not want to make her uncomfortable therefore ignored and I got so engrossed in conversation that I forgot about my anxiety and she kept me curious to know about her more therefore I offered her to accompany me to the library if she has no other commitment for the day to which she agreed happily.

I wanted to take a taxi but she asked me not to, "this is the place people walk to watch the majesty of the city, this is like the heart of the city and it is just a km away from here, let us walk, you would like it".

Though I was still not convinced knowing my health issues, I still agreed to her. We crossed the road and she brought me to the iconic Victoria Terminus, It stood right in front and no wonder it was the reflection of age old beauty. Structure always attracted and the massiveness amazed me, about everything, events that would have led to its formation and people who made it possible.

The weirdest thing was I had still not asked her name and neither did she, we somehow did not feel the need to know each other's name or what we do. Still it was so comfortable exploring together. I was very tired of all the walking as I was not so used to walk lately so I sat on a bench across the pavement, took a sip of water, she read the discomfort on my face and assured it was just around the next block and I smiled at her. We sat there for a while watching people, watching the stark difference of lives. This was the costliest place of the city with people from all walks of life, there were people in suits, in rags, with businesses around and there were people begging on the street. The sight around was peaceful yet disturbing on such biased distribution of resources in the world.

We got up and walked, after a few steps, she spoke in a very low voice, "I don't think it is a good idea to hang around with me or take me to the library".

My instinct response was "why what happened, why are you so low all of a sudden." I thanked her for helping me out of my anxiety attack and explained her about my issue, that had it not been her to my rescue I would have to be taken to hospital and it all would have been a great mess. I thanked her for understanding my condition and coming for my help without even caring who I was. "This world is still full of good people and you are one of them," I told her in an enforcing manner.

She smiled back at me, "I am happy to help but even you offered to take me to the library without knowing who I was, so even you are among those good people that you mentioned."

That's sweet of you and we walked ahead.

The massive building was right before us, it had unlimited number of staircase as seen from a distance. It just looked like a capitol structure from the time of Julius Caesar. I read it when I was in the school but was as fresh in my mind as I have once lived it, this impact of literature was because of the teacher we had in our class, Mr.Donald who was a teacher of conscience, he made every scene and act come live in our minds, he was one of my favorite teacher and I dedicate my love for literature to his amazing method of teaching, creating love for the subject.

We walked the never ending stairs and reached the entrance, she hesitated and said you just come while I wait here for you. I was confused and thought why she would not go inside having come this far so I insisted her to accompany. I could notice her fidgeting and attempts to cover herself with her scarf. I asked her to stay calm, "this is just a library and you need not to be scared of anything, no one would say anything to you".

You would not understand, they will not allow me get inside, I know.

I assured her, " please come with me, I am here."

She stayed behind me while I made the entry in the register, the watchman asked for the identity card and I flashed my Pan card. He asked for her too. I held her hand and entered confidently explaining she is with me and added the entry as plus 1. We entered and she was relaxed by now.

I wanted to ask about her fear but we got mesmerised of age old set up of the interior, smell of old books and British styled table chair arranged in rows. The fans were hanging on a huge rods travelling all the way from one end of the tomb to reach the convenient distance to make a difference. There were students lined up in silent sharing of knowledge between book and their soul. The silence was so loud that I felt our sign language would also make enough sound to disturb the peace around. We sat there for a while just watching and checked some of the book while all the time she just followed me without touching anything.

She sat there and watched in awe just like I did but soon got sleepy and she laid her head down on the table, I knew how infectious sleep is in that environment so decided to leave before everyone starts falling down in slumber. I shook her and we signed out the register.

The moment she stepped out, she freaked like a child, "I never knew libraries were of such kind, so peaceful that I wanted to sleep. I wish I could come here often and get peaceful sleep". I smiled and explained how library is not the place to sleep because if she did, everyone around her would feel the same and get distracted from their studies.

She seemed happy and repeatedly thanked me; there was something different about her which I was not very sure of. I wanted to ask about her life, about her family and life but could not gather enough courage to do so.

We sat down on the stairs of the building to talk and relax. Before I could ask anything she said, "I have never met anyone like you; you are the one who did not judge me for my looks, my dress up or my behaviour. I am not one from you; I do not belong to this society.

I was still confused but I asked her not to think that way, we all are one human being and we all belong to the same society, rich or poor, able or not able. Since she had told me about not been able to go to school I thought she must be from a not to do well family therefore she is spotting out the difference.

So I explained her how money is not the only thing that matter in our life, we might have little but we should live happy in that and find purpose to our life. After all love respect and family is all that matters.

"I don't have either of those. No family, no respect, no love, all I have is little money to survive. I do not belong to this city either; I was a small girl when I was brought here by my buaji after my parents passed away. She helped me get a job of baby sitting in a very big house; they were kind people but at times got violent on mistakes that I made. But I never left because where else would I have gone, I settled to my destiny. I didn't even realise when I turned 19 and fell for a man who was a sweeper in the same building, he was so much in love with me. I used to feel like a heroine from those Bollywood movies, we went out on dates at Juhu beach, he also promised to marry me and take me along with him. That was the happiest moment of my life so far."

I didn't want her to stop as I wanted to know everything about her, "so what happened next when everything was so beautiful, what went wrong?"

"My fate went wrong, that was the night when I was about to elope with him, he had promised to take care of everything, I packed my bag and stayed up whole night to get a knock at the door but he never turned up. I went back to my normal chores once again, still expecting explanation from his side but he did not ever come on his duty and I had no other point of contact so I almost lost my hope. My mistakes got more frequent and so the violence, I still stayed there hoping maybe someday he would come and take me out of this. Munto was not a bad man; he was in love with me so deeply that there was not even a single day he would leave the building without seeing me. He was also planning to get a mobile phone for me to stay in constant touch."

So did he come back for you? I interrupted her again.

"Yes after a month he came back and we eloped, we started living in a chawl in Malad. It was a one room house but that was the entire universe to me. I could sleep as much as I liked for the first time in my life, I did what I liked, I cooked for us and everything was so beautiful out from a Bollywood movie. But our happiness did not last long when a woman knocked my door on one rainy morning. Munto was out for work; I welcomed her and asked who she was. She was holding a child in her arms who was hardly of a year old, she sat on the ground and asked for a glass of water, I gave her water and she drank in a go. She then answered me "I am what you are". I was too innocent to understand what she meant so I asked her to tell her who she was in real. After listening to every word she spoke I broke in tears and so was she, my beautiful world came crushing down. She was the wife of the love of my life, holding his child in her arms begging me to get out of my own house. She waited until Munto came back, he was taken aback as his lies and dupes were out in public, he denied any relation with me and pushed me out of that house. Suddenly I had nothing and no one; I didn't even have the courage to go back to my employer. I wandered on the streets of Malad for the entire night looking for a place to hide as I was very scared of drunken men. I saw a group of women sleeping on one of the section of the pavement, it gave me little confidence and tried to lie beside them, just then a very fat lady woke up and screamed at me to go away. I went near to her and she looked at me from head to toe, I explained her whole condition after which she agreed to allow me there. I took a corner and slept for a few hours that were left for the sun to shine, hardly I knew that was the night after which the sun would never shine again in my life.

I was awaken by the same fat lady who asked me where would I go now to which I had no answer so she asked me to follow her, I followed her and from there on I am just following to whatever she asks me to. I work as an on call prostitute and go places wherever I am asked to. So there is nothing left, no respect, no family, no love in my life."

I was in tears even though I wanted to stay strong, what else she could have done in that situation, she wouldn't have survived or may be raped already if she didn't find that lady on that night. I could feel the pain she was in and that was the time I was the most helpless person on earth for I could not change anything in her life, all I could do was feel bad, very bad for her. Here I was suffering from depression and anxiety with all the comforts of my life and here she was, struggling to survive still standing so strong.

I did not know what to tell her, how to console her, consoling would have not changed her truth, I was not even able enough to help her out in any way, I wanted to offer her some money but at the same time did not wish to hurt her self-respect. I held her hand and asked her to stay as strong as she was and work for her future now as we never know what tomorrow would bring along and things would change for good. I knew these words are words alone but that was all I could offer.

"I am glad you considered me a friend and found me trustworthy enough to share your story with me; I forced a smile on my face. You can call me Nuha."

She thanked me again and I shared my contact with her and asked her to stay in contact as friends, she was very happy about being friends and it satisfied me a little as I had something to offer. She waved me goodbye screaming her name, I am Chamak, remember my name.

How could I have ever forgotten that name, Chamak. I dropped the plan to visit my dad and took a taxi back home while the return train ticket rested in my wallet. I asked the taxi driver to take me via Worli sea-link, I wanted to sail in my thoughts and feel the wild wind of this city on my face.

Chamak was the same wild wind of the city, "Victim of Destiny".

— x x x —

Chapter - 11

Social Work

Chamak was like a revelation to my life, my helplessness in her case made me cringe at my inability do anything, it disturbed me every day there on. Her weary yet hopeful eyes, her dimpled million dollar smile started haunting me and I could not stop myself from sharing this encounter with Falak. I waited that day for her to return so that I could explain her everything in much detail, just like Chamak did.

Falak was tired still she listened to everything I had to say, after which she said to me just one thing and that changed my life forever.

"So what have you thought to do about Chamak?" she asked

"It's sad as I couldn't do anything for her", I replied in my helplessness.

"Listen Nuha, there are a number of women even in the worst of conditions than Chamak, who are struggling for their survival, who are exploited and become the victims of all kinds of violence. And here you are with resources, education being your greatest asset, read about it, work for them, educate them. Find a purpose of your life, maybe this incident was on purpose to give you a direction. If nothing, at least take a step to share knowledge, we have a slum community right behind our building, why don't you go there and teach the kids. Education is the solution to address every problem of the individual and family as a whole."

Her words were true but I had no idea to take the first step, I searched online for things I could do or organisation that I could volunteer for but it seemed a very long process therefore I went to the community all by myself the very next day. It was two block far and I walked all the way, reaching there I was blank, it is situated at the foot hills of the western ghats, they engaged in growing vegetables on the hills and women worked as domestic help at those high rise buildings and their community had a small market where one can find everything from fishes to cloths. It looked like a self-sufficient community; I approached a shopkeeper who was trying to counts the sacks of potatoes in his shop. I asked the address for any school nearby, he readily pointed his finger towards small huts lined in a row, the school was behind those houses. I took the path and walked for 10 minutes to reach the entrance of the school, it was at the juncture of hill and plain, the ground of the school opened to massive mountain in front. It was beautiful but ill maintained, the roof of the school was of tin which heated the classrooms to extreme during full sun shine. I went to the office and found an old man dozing off on his chair. I knocked at the door and he woke up at once, I introduced myself to him and explained the purpose of my visit. He was silent for a minute and then spoke in the most innocent tone, "dear child, we do need a teacher but we cannot pay you."

I smiled at him and said, "Sir I do not want payment for the job, I want to volunteer as a teacher." He understood and we discussed about number of problems faced by the children there, lack of teachers, books, dropout rates as they are generally engaged in daily jobs at shops or fields. He took me around the three classroom school with a huge field, after that he took me to a class where I was introduced as their teacher. And they wished me in a rhythmic pattern "Goodmorning Ma'am" like we used to sing in our school times. There was no looking back after that.

Gradually I got in touch with the parents of children and thus engaged with women, I began visiting community on weekends where there were times when all we did was sit and talk about daily problems with women of the community, problems in their businesses, price rise, problems in marriage, domestic violence and we even laughed together on fashion trends and Bollywood flicks. Bollywood is definitely one of the life-line of the people of suburbs in Mumbai, they eat, talk, walk, sleep Bollywood, such impact it leaves on their lives. It was not that I was bringing any significant change in their lives, I was just trying to be the part of their daily life and understand them closely, their perspectives on things and problems they faced. I never did anything, even when we organised cleanliness and sanitation camp to educate people about keeping their community clean, it was those women who participated actively and talked about measures they could take to maintain cleanliness. I was just a person who would suggest ideas and they were the ones who planned and executed.

Things were going good, I had built a close relationship with them and in the process I was being healed, my anxiety decreased and there were things to keep me busy, there were things to think, plan and discuss. It was like they were the ones working for my betterment and re-constructing my soul.

It is when I took up writing back in my life, I started updating my blog once again, the same blog that I used to write in my school and college days about love and relationships, about weird feelings that creeps in teenage lives. This time it was with a purpose, I took to write about social problems, issues that plague our communities in day-to-day life, I wrote about things that hurt, about beautiful things that we never notice. Soon I gained enough readers and that paved a new beginning to my writing career.

By this time I had a whole set of community and direction to work for and a platform to express my thoughts on a larger scale. It helped me understand the general perspective of many people thus giving right path to any solution to a said problem.

Gradually my life was directed from insecurity and relationships to people and problems and throughout the phase Ryan supported me with all he could. From 24/7 conversation it came down to long night chats, but I made sure I share every detail about my work and things that I did, he might not be very interested to listen to all those not so interesting things after his long working hours at office but he did listen patiently to everything I had to share.

I was happy about everything in my life at that point, I was working though not earning, I was in a relationship with my ideal man who never hindered any of my dreams or choices, supportive of my career, my appearance, clothes, my thoughts and for the person I actually was.

— x x x —

Chapter - 12

Drift Apart

Time passed and our relationship matured, well-adjusted to the long distance set up. But sooner the monotony crept in our relationship with same kind of schedule and no chances of seeing each other for months made me paranoid. Insecurities started building up, whenever I did not hear from him for long hours or whenever he did not show much interest to talk like on our initial days. I was being impractical and assumed events and fought for lack of concern from his side, I connected things with the real time issues and problems of relationship that I was observing in the community and in my friend's lives.

The fear of being dumped got into my system so bad that one night I asked him to leave as this long distance relationship was too difficult to bear for me. I typed a long message and sent to him. I was emotional and I couldn't help it. It said,

"Ryan, these days I am not feeling good, I find no concern from your side, you do not care for me enough even to ask how I am doing for the whole day, I understand it is your work but so is mine, so it was in the beginning. I wait endlessly for your reply and even if you revert it is just the answer to my question. Why we are even together in this charmless relationship, please tell me if you have lost your interest in me."

After a long wait he replied,

"Are you in your mind, I reply to your messages right after I read it and never ignore it, what should I do when there is lot of work pressure that I am unable to give time. I am also here in a long distance relationship but I do not complain ever."

"You are taking me wrong, I was not complaining, should I not share what I feel, how different we have become since we first met."

"Things do not remain as they be in the beginning, situation changes, people change and we get used to each other, we do not have same level of curiosity or urge to talk as we have in the beginning."

"So you mean love fades with time?"

"See how you misinterpret my words; your overthinking is just ruining this relationship."

"Then I guess I don't want to be in this relationship knowing love fades so by the time we are married there will be no curiosity left to even look at me."

"I don't know Nuha what is wrong to your mind, may be you are right we should part ways right here."

"Okay, Good luck." I took not even a minute to reply this.

I kept my phone aside and wrapped myself around the pillow to sleep, trying not to think about it. Two hours passed, the phone clock flashed 2.05 a.m. but my mind did not rest to sleep, the torment of separation played with my confused mind. I loved him and how could I have let my love go away from me just like that. I picked my phone to dial his number and how I wished I would have never dialed it. It said, "the number you are calling is on another call, please wait or call again later", this was the worst nightmare coming true. I wanted to calm myself giving explanations to my mind that he might be on some emergency call otherwise who would he talk to at midnight after fighting with me. It could be any friend also with whom he must be discussing our problems in relationship, there were number of explanation but the mind was over powered with one strong assumption, what if it is the other woman because of whom he was unable to give me his time and concern.

I dialed again and this time his number was switched off, another thing that came in my mind was maybe it was some cross connection and his phone would be actually switched off because he was mad at me. I tried to convince myself with logic and illogic the whole night but in vain. How I wished he was near to me so that I could just see him and make things okay, just clear my doubts and relax my heart and mind.

That night my heart ached as all the doors to him were shut and there was no way I could make him talk to me, it hurts when you crave for something so bad and there is no way to address the same. I regretted for not apologizing to him for my misconception about his love although I was not sure if it was a meager misconception or he really had lost interest in me yet I felt apologizing would have been much better option than being in this total shut out. I did not sleep and tried his number after intervals knowing he wouldn't get up to switch on his phone.

In my mind, I was already heartbroken and in my heart I was deep in his love, for once I thought this was the end, and that too for such stupidity of mine

It was 9.00 a.m. when I dialed again, it was a relief to hear it ring at the other side, I waited patiently for him to answer but he did not. I left several messages asking him to talk to me. I was not sure why was I being so desperate to talk to him, I believed I was in love and sometimes we lose everything in the process of loving someone, including our self-respect and reason to rational.

After another hour of wait he finally answered,

"I slept last night after talking to a friend, I am sorry I was not in a good mood after all that so did not answer your call."

"That's okay; I just wanted you to know that I can't lose you at any cost"

"Then you should learn to trust me and my love", he replied

"I do and I will, pardon my insecurities, I will work on it"

I did not cross questioned him, even though I wanted to so bad, I was rather scared of my abandonment so I agreed to his words.

Because when I first fell in love, I was so sure about all the butterflies feeling and passionate kiss and longing to see each other that I had thought this was it, what takes for two people to live a relationship forever in life, that was what it demands to be in that bond of togetherness. I had concluded love was the property of us because we existed together and hence the love; that was where love originated for me for the first time. Gradually, time crept in, and with the passage of time in the relationship, that feeling of belongingness got rusted, my first forever ended with a revelation of time. I was not ready to rust this relationship with another formidable decomposer in the form of distance and misconceptions.

I agreed to him easily because I wanted to make stories together, build castles of passion in the struggle of survival and experience extremes of ecstasy and morose, I wanted to know what breaks me and what fixes me back, I wanted to fight passionately and love intensely. I wanted to experience and learn things, not by observation but by living it, playing it and owning it all. I wanted him to stay in my life as he was.

After this all I wanted was to end our long distance relationship and stay close where I could see him more often and even fight at times but without any distance, I was so scared after that crippled feeling of last night that I never wanted to feel that way ever again in my life.

I thought about it the whole day and did not message him that night as I was done being clingy all the time so thought to give it a rest. But life never misses a chance to play the game, the moment I was relaxed in my detachment I was pulled back to the same place. Ryan texted,

'Why can't we set ourselves on a path with an unknown destination and just get rid of the fear of being lost, live the moment to the most, enjoy what we have."

How was I supposed to take this line that seemed out of a movie dialog, was it a hint on the way he wants me, or the hint of bleak future we hold. I was not the person to settle for anything casual and here he was beautifying his diplomatic idea. Had I have reacted outrageously; it would mean I have become so negative that nothing good I see in anything. If I took it positively, that would mean I am up for this thing, whatever it is, a casual relationship veiled under the promises of living happy together. I was aware of the fact that the journey of a relationship without a direction is tiring and generally given upon. But the urge of acceptance drives us to do things we never intend to, speak what we never mean and settle for what we never want.

I decided to be positive about it and reacted like an ideal girl is expected to.

"Ryan, I was in search of a constant in my life like a homeless soul and I found my home in your heart, so everything you say or do that leads me to you is indeed a treasure in disguise. Let's live together the way you think is right."

"I love you Nuha, keep that trust in me. I want to be in your arms right now and love you until the day breaks."

How I wished it read until my last breathe instead of day breaks. I was still content as things were less cluttered on the front. I thought about things and it pained less, I wanted him to know how much I loved him and I wrote the goodnight message,

"Someday when you will be sitting among others, and I will be watching you from distant, smiling in my thoughts, how perfect you are, the innocent love of my teens, the one I am ready to spend my life with, my heart filled with pride flashing smile on my lips, I shall point at you and proclaim it loud–he is my man. Goodnight love."

— x x x —

Chapter - 13

Trouble in the Paradise

I was working with the community tirelessly on different issues; it became the most important aspect of my life and little by little replacing the needy, dependent girl in me with a strong headed and opiniated woman. And when a woman transforms they are bound to create ripples even in the calmest sea.

It was the weekend, I was hooked on my phone with Ryan, we were discussing about how life shall change once we start living together, and I was in my happy mode looking forward to our fairy tale take off. He was equally excited about the idea of being together, but I somehow ruined the euphoria by asking an insecure question,

"What if we lose this charm once we start living together, at times you are so violent over phone on little differences, I fear things might become even more violent when we are together in person."

"Is there anything interesting and happy to talk about with you?"

"No, this is my fear and I want you to address it."

"I will not be violent but there are circumstances when people lose their cool." He said

"In my community, there is a woman, whose husband exploits her, abuses her physically and verbally on little things. Last time she was just talking to a shopkeeper and her husband pulled her grabbing with her hair and she got hurt on her forehead, I helped with first aid, I insisted her to lodge an F.I.R but she denied."

"I don't know that woman so I cannot say, who knows if her character was actually bad", he said

"What are you saying, let's say she is of any character, does she deserve to be treated like that. No human has any right over another; she has every right to live respectfully."

"I don't want to waste my time over this discussion, I am not that man neither you are that woman so give it a rest."

"I pity your selfish attitude, if nothing at least you could have shown some compassion for a victim of domestic violence."

"You know what, I am done, do hell with your work and let me have my weekend at peace."

"Sure", I messaged immediately

I accept I overthink many times, okay every time but thoughts are bound to arise in the evolving mind. I wanted to know his stance on that situation, It was saddening that I ruined our good moments and his mood but more than satisfying to put my opinion strong without worrying about consequences. Nothing feels so good than being right and standing for the right, it is fulfilling.

Our fights got more often as my life and opinion got firm day by day. I thought I was doing well while I did not realise I was becoming less desirable cautiously. He was distancing himself and I was constructing dreams of togetherness, being totally in love. I had come to terms that finally my life was settling; I had a direction to work through and a relationship to look up to. I wanted to take our relationship to next level and was also ready to speak about him at my family in spite of the differences we had. I was ready to face the worst with him being my side.

At 11 p.m. when he pinged me after work I was elated to share everything I was thinking about the whole day. So I texted him,

"Ryan, do you really love me, and do you really want me for your life?". I messaged

'Yes Shona, I do, I want you to be my lawfully wedded wife,' with a wink emoji.

I am very serious and want to talk to you something important.

And before he could reply I called him immediately.

"Baby, I want to tell you that I love you and want us to be together. Since everything is so good, I have thought to discuss about us to my parents but before that I need you to talk to your parents. This way at least we can ascertain the future of ourselves"

"I do agree with everything that you are saying but how do you expect me to tell it to my parents now, I am not yet settled in my life, I don't even have a promising job."

But you said, you want to get married to me. And I am not asking you to marry me the very next day, all I want is to talk to your parents about us so that I can do the same, it will take years to convince our parents anyway.

"I did say and I want to but not now or not even in recent future. I cannot talk to my parents about us"

Those words broke me, "Ryan, I want to get married to you because I want a life together not a partnership to share luxury in conjunction, I don't want to wait in the hope of collision to the perfect time, I want to dive in and unfurl life before it is too old. I want to marry young."

"But I am not ready to marry."

"How many times do I say we are not getting married this soon, it is just that I want this process to start to convince our parents because I am not among the ones who would like to sacrifice family and go beyond their wishes. However I want us to be together in the same light."

His excuses piled and found ever possible reason to escape this, I chose to disconnect the call, and he didn't care to revert either.

I was not sure if my expectation was wrong or his stubbornness, he was the one asking to marry and today he was the one freaking out on just the discussion of the same. I didn't know if the love diminished or I was no longer desirable enough. I was not able to comprehend well because I was always in the idea that marriage is like a union of two souls, where they grow together, learn and build careers together, unfold mysteries of possibilities and impossibilities in alliance, become the chorus of happy days and haunting nights while unfolding love each day.

But what love is it, where two people cannot be together for there are huge barriers of properties defined stronger than passion for one another, hidden in the beautiful cover of rationality and practicality of life. Why is it that we choose our rationality over every passion that blooms within the walls crafted by the modern architects in the veil of age-old ruckus? And they aren't wrong because someone said, there is nothing right or wrong, it is exactly what we want at that moment, our clear, well thought actions and decisions that we rationalise to be appropriate for that moment. And this was Ryan's well thought decision probably.

Although I was heartbroken, not knowing the direction to our relationship, I managed to wish him good night as my usual routine.

"When my hair turns grey and my face is wrinkled, there will be that one man who would find me beautiful, who would see that 22years old girl in me aged gracefully. That one man would make me his universe, love me for no reason and he would care like no one ever. That one man who would still bring smile on my wrinkled face, I wanted you to be that one man and you could not. Remember this Ryan that no love is absolute but the culmination of little of each part; love is the hope, care, respect and adjustments. Love you, Good night."

He did not reply to that either, which made me restless; I was not ready to end my perfect story, couldn't have afforded to give up just like that, it was painful, like the real physical pain, I could feel it in my heart. I compromised with my ego for my true love and here I was turning the most beautiful dreams of my life to the bitter reality. It made me wonder how the same thing made my life beautiful also made my life as miserable.

— x x x —

Chapter - 14

Delhi Days

Amidst all the fights and differences I decided to end this for once and all, not the relation but the distance. I was sure about us and wanted this to work, I discussed it with Ryan and he was more than happy with my decision to shift to Delhi. We had fallen in relationship being this far and our relationship continued long distance, this was not possible in the real world scenario where insecurities, mistrust devour even the best of the bonds. Surviving a long distance relationship is not always easy and it is almost impossible in a new relationship, therefore my decision of shifting to Delhi was on two fold motives, first was Ryan and second was to pursue my academics further in the area of my interest, social work being one of them.

Fortunately things went as planned and I was able to secure admission to master degree. Falak also changed her job and we came to Delhi, coming to Delhi was a refreshing change to life as this was the city I had first come to live after leaving Bhagalpur, my hometown. It was like coming to square one. This was the same city where I had lived the most memorable days of my life during my school and college days and it was the same for Falak, however she always prefer Mumbai over Delhi. I was happy as all my friends and close ones were here, even Samar was here, the backbone of my life, a mentor and a guide. Some relationship goes even beyond blood relationships, so was us. I respected the man he was and he adored me for the girl I was.

Above all I was happy being in my city, I was going to be able to see Ryan as and when I wanted to, to be close to him and give meaning to our relationship. This had to work as I had given my all, all my love and effort to make it real. Ryan was equally thrilled to live our moments more often rather talking about it all the time.

It was 13th February; we met over a reunion of our school mate, since all our friends knew about our history back in school, they were smitten to find that we were back together. I was never so vocal about my relationship with anyone but it was me taking a step forward to share my story to friends. The way we met, fell all over again and I even whispered my pretty dream to my school's best friend, Arpi who was now happily married. I whispered her, "I can't wait to start my life together with him."

She rolled her eyes and gave me the weirdest look, "since when have you started thinking in this direction, but nice that you sound sorted." I blushed, I was in love.

After our meet up he asked me on a date, he always wanted to ride on his bike with me, although bike scares me, I was okay to go along. All these time among friends we had only shared glances and not talked to each other. Sooner we were left alone, he smiled wickedly and said, "I don't believe you are here, right in front, with me, it is too good to be true." It was hard to believe for me as well but I had put so much of effort to be there was enough to make me realise the reality. I smiled and I could just do that.

Since I was away from the extreme winter of Delhi for so long, I had lost the power to cope, while I took the back seat on his bike, I shivered in the chilled wind trying to hide myself from the direct wind behind his broad shoulders. He was quick to notice so he dropped his speed and asked if I was comfortable. I nodded my head wrapped in shawl and he gave his mocking smile once again, tearing the chilly wind his voice rang, "you are still a baby."

"No I am not, I screamed back."

"Okay, if you are not, can you ride this bike as I am freezing to go further?"

"Oh! Yes I can do anything I want to", I gave him back and to my surprise he took the brake and the bike came to halt.

What happened, why did you stop? I asked.

"I want my not so baby girl to ride it while I relax behind."

"Are you kidding me? I am too scared to be here on the back seat, riding is impossible."

"Nothing is impossible, trust me", he said

I trusted him for everything so I took this plunge defying my fear, forgetting my anxiety.

Riding a bullet is difficult indeed but he instructed me in the beginning, to accelerate for speed and hit brake gradually by decreasing the speed first. Being a quick learner there I was, ripping through the chilled wind, my face numbed and my heart pounding fast in thrill and happiness of experiencing something unimaginable. It was 11.30 p.m. at night in the silent roads of Delhi, I was fearlessly riding a bullet with Ryan sitting behind. Definitely an unbelievable thing to do for a girl who was drenched in fear and anxiety, love does have the power to do wonders.

I did not speak for some time, as I was in my thoughts, when Adel had constantly killed my confidence by his negative comments on how I could never be the normal girl or how I didn't know to stay happy and how I was not even a girl as I did not behave like other girls he knew.

Ryan didn't speak either, probably allowing me to sink in the thrill of the moment. But then I saw a truck approaching and I freaked out, I screamed and Ryan immediately held the handle from behind, it was the loveliest moment life gifted me, I was allowed to be wild and fun while I had his back.

"Where are we going? This road seems never ending, I screamed again.

"Keep riding, I will tell you the stop."

So we stopped at a quiet but cute looking small dhaba on the road side. There were small yellow bulbs hanging on the branches of the giant peepal tree, round tables were carefully arranged under the shade of that tree with a contemporary lamp on each of the table. It looked dreamy, right out from one of my dreams of a perfect date.

Wow! Ryan this looks so beautiful, I exclaimed.

And he took me with my hand, pulled my chair and I took the sit.

"I didn't know you were that romantic a person", I took the dig

"Am I, No, It's just that this place was available at this time of the night."

And I looked at the watch, it was 11.55 p.m., Falak would kill me, I freaked out again so I thought to give her a ring. I called up and she was already half asleep, all I could understand was, "come home soon".

Ryan left to order something to eat and I waited checking on my phone, being out in Delhi this late was something to be worried about but I was with Ryan and that was all I could think of. I looked up away from my phone screen and saw Ryan coming with a cake, full of candles on it. I did not know the purpose; it was neither my birthday nor his, neither our anniversary nor any special reason to celebrate.

I gestured the question of why all this, he ignored and placed the cake before me, it read, "Be my Valentine", I saw that and tears came to my eyes, it was long I had forgotten things like these, I didn't even realise the significance of 12 a.m. 14th February. He was too shy to handle the moment and to hide his embarrassment he asked me to cut the cake quick as he was too hungry. I was in the moment, looking at him, admiring for the little effort he took just to bring a smile on my face. I knew how shy a person he was, doing this all just for me definitely made me the most special person. I hugged him and he ignored that too, avoiding the moment, he was trying to hide something but I succeeded to snatch that too, it was a pink greeting which read,

"This is my first valentine that I have celebrated in my life and from today I wish to celebrate every valentine with you. Be my forever."

It was the only romantic moment of my life out from a fairy-tale, I wanted to live the most of it but my body was turning numb due to strong freezing wind, my hands and lips started shivering as I tried to speak, cheeks turned red and my palms were white. He immediately came to my side and hugged me tightly assuring nothing has happened, I sunk my head in his jacket and he kept me holding for long, rubbed my palm and feet until I was stable a little. I was covered under layers, his jacket, scarf everything on me. He kept holding my hand and I looked into his eyes and spoke my heart out, "I love you, and I want to love you just like this forever."

If moments could be relived again and again, I would have chosen that valentine's night, he made me fall for him and I couldn't help but fall because in the long time I was not given a choice to be wild and yet be loved. This was the reason I was so sure about him that he is the one, the one I want to live my life with.

I was also supposed to be happy ever after from the day Ryan rescued me from the inner monster of sorrow, introducing me to the world full of dreams and hopes. I was eager to finish my degree and get married to the love of my life, every day we had the never ending chats on our long lists of things to do in life together. We still fought on hypothetical reasons as the real cause of our fight being distance was now gone forever.

Since I had taken such a big step I wanted him to give our relation some assurance by discussing with our parents as it was always important for me, I was an insecure person in the relationship because I feared what is more, and he was rather composed about things like these. Being in depression for two years definitely had changed my personality and had made me more paranoid on little things, I wanted to assure things before it was ruined by any other external factors. Hardly had I realised that if a relationship ends, it was meant to no matter what assurances you get from any of the side, like marriages break too. There is no security bigger than love for each other, because it is only love that keeps a relationship alive, love protects each other and no other thing can save the bond.

It was a Friday evening, I was as usual reading articles on Feminism, it pointed out very important aspect of feminism, that a woman should stand for a woman as they expect a man to stand for a woman and I couldn't agree more, if women are united and stand for each other, who can dare touch us or exploit us. But in the real life scenario, women disses women too, jealousy and outsmarting each other interests people more than things like taking a stand, unity or fighting for the right. We seem to be so occupied with our lives that we do not even care to know what is happening at the door next. I was engrossed in my thoughts when I received a text.

"Are you Nuha?"

I generally do not reply to an unknown number but my true caller showed a woman's name, Ankita. I was just going through the lesson of feminism and I thought there is no harm in asking the matter so I replied,

"Yes, Nuha here, what is the matter and may I know who are you"

"I am Ankita, I want to talk to you something personal but only if you trust me."

"Yes Ankita tell me, shall I give you a call"

"Yes please."

I called her immediately and there was a faint voice of a girl sobbing, it really disturbed me, she was a total stranger to me and I did not know how to react to that situation.

"Hey please tell me what is the matter and why do you want to talk to me, I don't even know you.'

"But I know you, you are Nuha from Ryan's school mate and you guys are together now."

This sentence of her turned my face red and all my senses were alert, "yes we are together, what do you want to say."

"I just wanted to let you know that Ryan is cheating on you, while he is with you, he keeps on texting me to get back in relationship with him, and I am his ex. Even though I have moved on with my life, he doesn't leave a chance to try on me and send me messages of our old times and how badly he needs me."

These sentences from her came as a blow to my life, like someone has just hit me hard on all my senses and I have lost all the ability to reason or interpret. I was not yet sure about everything that she was speaking about so I collected myself and a rather rude tone questioned her,

"What are you saying, this can't be true and why should I even trust you on this, you are just another stranger to Me." just before this I was being a proud feminist and now I was not even ready to trust a woman who was trying to share something.

"I will send you the screenshots of his messages and calls that he had made to me", that came as a halt to me, I was not left to counter that any further, even though I was perplexed I was not wanting to know about those screenshots, how could I have, but how could I have not, someone was trying to ruin my head and I needed to know it, investigate it and dig the truth out. I disconnected her call immediately and my phone showed two new messages in the notification just after that.

My hands had already turned cold and my mouth was dry, I wanted to believe it was all fake and made up, one thing I didn't want was this, I had not even dreamt it in my distant dream. I was the one always freaking out on the thought of break up or things going wrong in relationship but I never mistrusted Ryan, I never doubted him for even once.

I opened her messages to read his messages to her and it clearly read, these were the messages of Ryan to Ankita,

"I miss our good old times shona, please meet me for once, I miss you."

"I was thinking about you shona, you are always in my mind."

"Please please meet me."

I collapsed on the ground with tears in my eyes, I didn't know what to do next, who to call, what to say, I was shattered into pieces once again in life. My pretty dreams were broken into pieces and its poignant clamour jingled in my ears. I was cheated all along the time while I was considering those as the most beautiful times of my life. I was cheated when I was preparing my mind to get married to him. I was cheated while he was promising eternity to me, I was cheated while I was feeling secured in his arms, I was cheated when he promised to celebrate every valentine of his life. The colossus of everything that I had believed in came falling down bit by bit and there was nothing I could do.

I still did not lose my hope there; I had the courage to call him, his phone rang for 8 times and he did not pick up his call, this was when I was bound to doubt everything that was happening. So I called his sister and she informed Ryan was out from home since noon, I generally know about his whereabouts but this was something new, just then I called him again and he picked his call.

"Ryan, where are you?"

"Home, shona, I was sleeping."

"No you are not at home", and I disconnected his call as it was too much to handle, knowing he was lying on my face, he was lying about his love for me, his commitment and I was just being the fool at the hands of destiny.

I called the girl, Ankita,

"Is he with you right now?", I enquired

"No he is not"

"He lied to me that he was home while he is not as his sister already told me about it."

"Look Nuha, I know the kind of man he is, he wouldn't stick to a girl, who knows he must be with some third girl and we don't have any idea about it."

"Why did you tell me all these?", I asked with tears in my eyes

"Because I didn't want a girl like you to be the victim of his dupe"

"Well, I already am. Thanks by the way."

It would not be enough if I say I was heartbroken, I could hear my soul crying in pain and my life flashed back before my eyes, all my right and wrong decisions that had brought me to the place I was. For that single moment I regretted for walking out from Adel, but it also reminded me of the suffocated feeling he made me go through and I brushed that thought off. What difference it made, Adel or Ryan, both of them took away my hope in some or the other way, both cheated on me, one with the idea of a perfect woman and the other with another woman. I was never loved for the matter of truth. But all these were just a reason given to calm down my inner storm; the fact was I was left devastated.

After all these, I still had a slight doubt on the girl who just broke the bubble of my fairy-tale, I wanted to know the truth but from his own side so I repeatedly called on Ryan's number while still sitting on the floor crying profusely. He answered the phone after fourteen rings,

"Hello, he spoke in a drowsy tone."

"Wake up please; I know you are not sleeping."

"What the hell, I am home, he said in his agitated tone."

"I know you were not home so please stop this game right away and meet me now, I ordered."

"Okay, I will be there in an hour."

I could see him from a distance sitting on a bench outside the coffee shop while I walked towards him, how different it was today, same step that was always swift towards him was heavy and unwilling at this time. I wanted to confront and the same time I did not want to hear the terrible truth that would confirm my reasons of hatred and I would be left with nothing but pain.

He stood up to pull my chair; I stopped him and took my seat. Before I could say anything he was already on his knees.

"Shona, I don't want anything, there are many misunderstanding between us due to our miscommunication. Please understand. I always wanted you and only you, please let us get married."

'You sure you love me? I asked in my composure'

'Of course I do, you have been the only love of my life.'

'If that was so, what was the need to contact another girl, coming this far into our relationship? What was the need to miss her and ask her to be in relationship? Was I not enough Ryan?'

'Please Shona, listen to me, and let me explain.'

'Explain what, your lies and cheating and fake promises.'

He was silent after that; I could read that helplessness in his eyes, he was sorry for everything he had did and that was more than fine to me but I don't know why, I could not gather enough courage to give one more chance.

Tears rolled down my cheeks, I was helpless not knowing what next, just then he held my hand and pulled me with him, he was walking swift in anger and I was resisting going ahead, it looked like a child is being dragged by his mother. I yelled at him to leave my hand but he did not so I had to follow him, we boarded the taxi and I sat close looking at him in surprise, he was fierce, he never looked so stern and determined ever. I had no idea what was he up to but I still followed without any further question as I knew he was mad and helpless inside. The taxi stopped right at the gate of his house, this was where I lost my cool and I resisted going inside. He asked me to step out of the taxi multiple times and I denied. Observing this commotion the driver prompted, "madam ji maan jaiye sir ki baat, ladaiya to har rishte me hoti hain." In my embarrassment I got down the vehicle without wasting a minute, once again he held my hand and marched forward.

I was not knowing how should I react to this, how should I go in front of his family. He was certainly not in his senses, clearly inviting trouble for himself but there was nothing I could do to stop him. He ringed the call bell of his door and my heartbeat raced that is when I wanted to run away and hide somewhere. I asked him to leave my hand at least so that we could meet in a less threatening manner. As his sister opened the door he released my hand immediately. I knew his sister as we were all from the same school once, she welcomed me with a bright smile and I forced a smile too. I stepped inside with a huge commotion in my mind and took a seat there in the living room while staring at my hand that had got red finger marks and it looked awful. I wondered what was he doing, of course I was shocked but it was somewhere relaxing too, it was an assurance that he loved me; I could feel his love for the first time in his anger, helplessness and stubborn eyes. Could it be love?

He introduced me to his mom while she gave me a scanning look from head to toe like every mother would look at the girl her son would introduce to and I was the first for her. I bowed a little and greeted her, she asked me to sit and we talked where all I did was answered. She was a lovely woman indeed like every mother would be, curious and inquisitive to know about the girl who could be her prospective daughter in law. It was calm by now, although I was in lot of confusion, my heart still skipped a beat every time I stole a look at him, and he was sitting like a responsible man, man I have always wanted to be with.

After the short conversation I asked to take a leave, his mother asked me to visit again and I walked out. From there it became even more complicated for me; from here I was not sure which way to go this time. To trust or not to.

He held me in his arms and asked me to love me once more and that he would change everything for good but all I could respond was stare into his eyes that was once my fairy town. I was so deep in love that I did not get any chance to think anything else other than being together. And today when he stood so wrong I still tried to justify him in my mind, I was blaming myself for not been able to give my love completely, there were times when I was unsure about our future and freaked out, may be those were the times he might not have wanted me and ended up contacting other girls. But this justification of my heart failed to convince my brain and here again I was trapped in a tussle of my mind and heart.

He did love me otherwise I wouldn't have been so convinced of his love but then his action spoke a different story. It might be that he was so in need of attention and acceptance that when things were not going well between us he looked for that at other places but how ethical was that. When a human heart is driven by need, that is when they lose control over conscience and cross the thin line of ethic and non-ethic, this was the extent that I wanted him that I came up with reasons of his unacceptable behaviour.

I spent days in distress until I could take it no more; his words ringed my ears, "let's get married". I started thinking that may be once we get married, things will get better, we shall live together, and there will be no space to other things except love. I reasoned to myself day and night thinking the same, trying harder to give my love one last chance. His continuous messages did make me more vulnerable and I gave in.

After a month of complete avoidance I could not do it anymore so I agreed to meet and talk about us. I was happy that I would get to see him but equally paranoid about things that I would end up doing for we do not use brain when heart does the talking.

He was waiting for me and the moment he saw me coming, he rushed to hug me, I couldn't stop him, I was there in his arms searching for peace and home to my chaotic mind but I did push him away and we sat without speaking a word. After he cheated on me, ideally, I should be the one to collect my pieces and never look back but here I was surprising to myself, I spoke first and what I spoke was the proof that we lose our ability to reason out in love.

'Ryan, I want to marry you, soon.'

'What? Soon? Are you kidding me?'

'No I am not, here is the phone, I will call my parents and you call yours. Let us end this stupidity and give a direction to our relationship. Let's get married.'

'But I am not yet settled; I told you already, I can't do it'

'I am with you, together we can work and find out ways for ourselves, it is not that people who marry soon don't make good careers.'

There was a silence, silence that could choke you and eat you alive. That was when I rolled myself in a bundle of morose and walked away. I was in tears, unstoppable tears, my throat was filled and every step that I took, how I wished he would just stop me and ask me to say "I Do".

He did leave me in pieces, pieces I could never collect back.

You need that courage to walk out
Walk out of where you don't belong
Walk out of things not meant for you
Walk out of relationships you don't need
Walk out of situations not comfortable
And then walk out of the crowd
To create you as you want

My hope on love shattered forever, that very day I gave up my pretty dream because some dreams are too pretty to live.

— x x x —

Chapter - 15

Transformation to a Woman

All these times I was in belief that one right man, one beautiful start, one magic wish will mark the beginning of my happily ever after. I was in belief that my happiness shall then find the way but in due course of time, I saw many charming prince losing the throne one by one and in the process I conquered myself step by step and this was my first step.

For the period of four months, there was not a single day I did not stalk him, I stalked, I craved, I wished to run back into his arms but this time I allowed my conscience to control my heart. I worked day and night on cases that were part of my curriculum in Social Work, I wanted to get engrossed so much that nothing should matter and somehow I succeeded, partly because of his complete disappearance and partly because of my valued self-respect. I worked with the kids helping them to get enrolled in schools, worked with women to get legal help and take a stand against the domestic violence they suffer at home. I tried everything to keep myself away from the thoughts and pain of heartbreak.

On the nights that haunted me of the lost stories of my life, all the reasons worth enough to abandon me, all the fake promises done million times by men of my life, gave me sleepless nights and drenched pillow. None of my stories made it to the altar I dreamt of once, none of the men of my lives could stand by my side. What hurt the most was the fact how well I was aware of my own contribution to broken heart, my flaws. And here I was asking women to take a stand for themselves while I myself was faltering over heartbreak. I was motivating women, sharing hope to fight back against their gruesome stories while I was being drifted towards hopelessness. I could have not let that happened to me, how could I, I had a dream to live by this time, many women and children who looked up to me. This was enough motivation for me to stand back on my wobbling feet and take the responsibility for myself and for all the lives I could make little differences in.

And one day I found Ryan has moved on with one of his ex. I already knew this that Ryan was not the man who would go beyond his limits to save the relationship, he was the one who would replace me and he did. It did not hurt me somehow as I was glad because, becoming the other woman in someone's life was the worst nightmare for me, the lowest point where I never wanted to find myself, I was better off heartbroken.

I just watched how quickly his once eternal love worn out in a few days. I tell you, beware of this feeling called love, and even more beware of the cosmic promises exchanged. You never know who speaks in the process, whether it is him or his short lived testosterone.

No wonder the pain of unrequited love is worse than any physical pain but living respectfully is more important than loving explicitly. That was the day I wrote my first blog for every woman who somehow does not allow their reason to win over their emotion and chose to become the other woman. The blog said,

"*Dear Women,*

I left the person I loved because I was afraid I will become the other woman someday". I chose to walk away because I value myself more than anything. I profess to choose oneself over everything even for the millionth time and all over again because if you exist, so is everything else. There is a universe in you, a complete universe which is capable enough to exist in its singular form, nothing less than that.

If I own such a massive universe within, imagine my ability, my potential and infinite unexplored possibilities and capabilities trapped within, I am ought to be the supreme of I, and why would someone like that settle for any less. If I allow myself to be the other woman in someone's life that is when I admit that I am less. And I am not less, I know every spec of what I am made of and I am not less. I would not lose my self-respect and chase after someone because then I will lose my identity. I am in the control of my choices and I will choose the best and the best would not put you to become the other woman.

There is just one person, who would stay with you right from your adversity to your prosperity. He would surround your life in such a way that you would be glad and willing enough to allow him to be the intruder in your universe. As you will be the only woman in his life.

P.S. Never chose to be the other woman, ever, because there is nothing called "I love you but..."

In an effort to save others I was being saved, writing saved me from dissipating in oblivion. And I fell in love with this, with something for the very first time that would not leave me ever. My life time companion.

When life hits you, it hits you from all the distant corners, while I was struggling to fix myself back and finding a way to sustain the ache, my haunting past came back in my worst.

Adel messaged me that day while I was on my way to the field work in the community,

"What goes around comes around, you left me for the person who left you for someone else, that's how you should be paid with, I am happy."

Reading this my heart broke; how can someone find their happiness in somebody's tears. I had just deboarded metro at Kashmere Gate, which is the busiest metro station of Delhi, I seemed to be lost in the crowd, it suffocated me and I ran towards the exit. I wanted to escape from everyone and everything; I did not want anyone to look at me as the loser I have been in this game of love and life. I settled myself on a secluded bench outside the station, took a sip of water and sat there watching people, their rush to reach somewhere. I was lost in my thoughts once again, pacifying my heart and reasoning all the decisions to make sense. I was alone and I was scared I might be pushed into another anxiety episode, to obstruct my mind from any further thought, I called mom immediately.

Hello, she spoke.

Mom, what are you doing?

What happened beta, all good?

To speak further I needed enormous courage, because the moment my voice break she would know and get worried. I tried my best to sound normal to assure that I was fine and was just missing her. But as we know no mom would just settle for that, she would dig it deeper to know exactly that has happened and she did the same.

I lost the track of time in our conversation, our discussion from daal khichdi of home to pollution of Delhi, it covered everything in between. She updated me of my friends getting married and who eloped with whom, how young generation has misconstrued the meaning of love and what not. And for the very first time she asked me,

'Beta, when are you thinking to get married? You can tell me if there is anyone you like, I will consider my daughter's choice.'

It didn't come as surprise to me, she is my mother, she will be the one knowing my heartfelt things even before I realise, I asked her in response,

'Ammi, how do we decide who we want to get married to, marriage is a serious thing.'

'We don't decide, we feel it, the right person would make you feel it.'

'And how do we know he is the right person.'

'Beta I didn't get the chance to fall in love and know the person before marriage so I can't tell you what happens before that but I can tell you what keeps the relationship going, it is the respect for each other, when you don't fear being with the person, when you trust enough to pull each other out of storms of life.' 'But remember one thing for sure, do not hold on to something that hurt you again and again, learn to let go things, life is to live.'

'You are right, okay Ammi I will go back home, talk to you later. Bye.'

'Take care beta'

I hung up, my chaotic soul was calmer now, cloudy thoughts were much clearer. I have definitely learned to cope up with anxiety over the years and it was satisfying. From here on I did not want anyone to affect my brain, my body and my life. I wanted to let go.

I reached home and wondered how Adel came to know about my break up with Ryan so I checked his Facebook page to get some idea, what I found was a lesson to learn.

He broke my heart and the first thing he did was to remove all my traces from his show business, a.k.a social media. All geared up for his next inning. And here I was wondering how mechanised love is. In a few days he erased the memories of years. I knew I was slow, I expected Juliet story in the age of Netflix and chill.

In my rage I replied Adel,

"Thanks, at least I could make you happy in some way.'

He was quick to attack me with his boxed up anger and he texted me back,

'A girl like you deserve such thing, I am still ready to accept you after all these, still ready to marry you.'

'That's quite a tempting offer Adel, would you really accept me after all these?"

'Yes, only if you come with a true heart and love me with all your heart, I still did not move on with any other girl.'

Adel was right, he was still waiting for me, he was loyal, honest and the man of his words but the only problem was that he was the blood child of patriarchy and wanted a woman who could be the victim of same. And I could have become the one, but it was too late now.

He was not wrong, he was true to his culture and his learning, and he was from the same society as I was, fed by patriarchy in the silver spoon. Same society that held marriage as the ultimate importance than education of their daughters, same school where by default school leader meant the boy student and secretary meant the girl student, captain meant the boy student and vice-captain meant the girl student. For once in my school time I started to believe that leader has a gender connotation and it belongs to male of the society but I evolved as a woman and he diminished in the age old ruckus of patriarchy.

So for the first time I decided to be very honest with him and I offered the proposal,

"I am a social worker and I will work for the society all my life, In shaa Allah. I will be out from my home working; I will be interacting to men and women without considering gender. Cooking, cleaning and washing are not my role; I will decide my roles according to my preferences so do not restrict your expectation to my roles in your mind. I respect your family culture but I will not fake anything that I am not before them, allow me my reality at every stage of life and I will respect. I have my sister's kids, Mithi and Maaz to look after and they are the most precious souls of my life, nothing comes before them, hope you will respect that. And you already know that I have anxiety, although I have learned to cope up with it there might be times I would go selfish and unreasonable, you will need to understand. And yes the most important thing, I don't want to give birth to a child but I definitely want to have children through adoption from orphanage, we can decide on numbers of adoption as per our income later. And there are orphans waiting for a home and family, I will be glad enough to provide as much as I can rather just create like everyone else.

Not having a child biologically have two major reasons, first I am already a mother to my sister's babies, giving their place to anyone is unimaginable and even if I would try to treat all the children equal in my mind, their innocent minds are bound to find a difference even if there is none, I cannot risk that, I cannot make them miss anything in the world or feel any less ever.

Secondly, struggling from anxiety for such a long period I have no courage to undergo such painful experience which is not only during the birth but also post birth, I do not think I will be a good care giver, I will ruin myself emotionally if I get attached to anything else in my life anymore. I have had enough and I want to give my best to what I have right in front and I want to take responsibilities of what I am capable.

These were the things I wanted you to know before you think of 'accepting' me.

So are you ready to marry me?"

There was no immediate response; he messaged after five long hours,

"Why should I sacrifice so much to be with you, I am a simple man and expect a simple thing, wife, children and a family? And what kind of a girl does not want to give birth, that is what they are meant for."

"Well, I am the kind."

After that he did not have the courage to message me and I was clear enough to never look back, I knew what I wanted from my life thereafter. That very day I received the acceptance letter from UNICEF and I walked away with a determination and a dream in my eyes.

I am not sad, I am not hopeless, I still believe in love and strongly believe the one who will love me will not just accept me for what I am but understand me for why I am and even if that never happens I am enough, I am the hope to hundreds of people who might need me even for just a smile or a ray of hope. My work would take me places, earn me people and bless me happiness. What more do I need.

That day I dressed up in my black Zara dress, red lipstick and
glittery eyes I wore blush on my cheeks and
diamonds in my loose messy hair

I set out to celebrate my success and a newfound
meaning, a meaning to my life

Leaving behind the battle of acceptance and assurance,
today I belonged to myself

Today I have love for what I am

I have learned life, and pain is the lesson most important
I have learned life and happiness is the chapter most read

I have fought back in every reel because you see;
I am a warrior in high heels

And I will bleed till I Lead

Dear Girls,

Do not accept to become the secretary or vice-captains when you have all the potential to become leaders and captains. Do not accept roles defined by others, do not do something just because someone wants you to, do what you want to, what your heart yearns for and what your soul calls for.

You will hop from relationship to relationship looking for love and acceptance in the times of hormonal surge and life instability. Let that wreck you to the rock bottom but when you reach that stage do not forget the buoyancy theory, bounce back with immense courage and reach for the sky. It is okay to expect fairytale love but do not wait to be rescued by anyone, rescue part was always wrong. Be the princess who knows to reign her territory.

There will be a time when your life might take such a turn where people start calling you names like a bitch, slut and a whore. Remember this then, a bitch is a female dog while slut and whore is a derogatory noun that reflects back the evils of patriarchy. It has absolutely nothing to do with you.

No matter what you go through, mental instability or personal issues never halt one thing and that is your education and continuous learning. An educated woman is like a lion roar which overpower every squeaks of the mighty jungle.

And yes don't hold on to a frog expecting him to turn to a prince, find your prince for real.

Yours
Nuha

— x x x —

As long as I am a woman,
My character is at stake
At the whims of my pursuer or the ones I pursue
I can be a bitch to some and whore to a few